**"In the worst-case scena
and somebody else gets**

"I don't need to remind you that the ambassador's thugs shot at us."

"Do you think they'd hurt Mom?" Mallory asked.

A long moment of silence stretched between them. In a quiet voice, he said, "Yes."

Deep in her gut, she knew he was right. Her mother could be killed. She clenched her fingers into fists, holding on to fragile hope. Sensing her distress, Elvis poked his nose between the front seats and bumped her elbow. She loosened her hand to stroke the soft fur on his head. The warm friendliness comforted her, though she was far from calm.

From the moment her mother went missing, Mallory feared dire consequences, even before she knew the whole story. "What can we do?"

"I know you don't want to hear this, but we should call the police."

But she couldn't betray Mom's confidence, couldn't be the person to send her to prison. "Before we call in the cops, we have to find her."

K-9 MISSING PERSON

USA TODAY Bestselling Author

CASSIE MILES

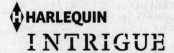

HARLEQUIN
INTRIGUE

For all the fantastic, talented K-9 dogs. And, as always, for Rick.

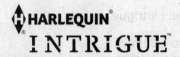

HARLEQUIN®
INTRIGUE™

Recycling programs
for this product may
not exist in your area.

ISBN-13: 978-1-335-59161-6

K-9 Missing Person

Copyright © 2024 by Kay Bergstrom

For questions and comments about the quality of this book, please contact us at CustomerService@Harlequin.com.

TM and ® are trademarks of Harlequin Enterprises ULC.

Harlequin Enterprises ULC
22 Adelaide St. West, 41st Floor
Toronto, Ontario M5H 4E3, Canada
www.Harlequin.com

Printed in Lithuania

MIX
Paper | Supporting
responsible forestry
FSC® C021394

Cassie Miles, a *USA TODAY* bestselling author, lived in Colorado for many years and has now moved to Oregon. Her home is an hour from the rugged Pacific Ocean and an hour from the Cascade Mountains—the best of both worlds—not to mention the incredible restaurants in Portland and award-winning wineries in the Willamette Valley. She's looking forward to exploring the Pacific Northwest and finding mysterious new settings for Harlequin Intrigue romances.

Books by Cassie Miles

Harlequin Intrigue

Visit the Author Profile page at Harlequin.com.

CAST OF CHARACTERS

Mallory Greenfield—Part owner of Reflections, an art gallery near Aspen, she's devastated by the disappearance of her mom.

Shane Reilly—Former award-winning skier, he's started a new career as a private investigator and is hired by Mallory.

Elvis—The black Labrador retriever with an Elvis-like sneer is K-9 trained for search and rescue in the mountains and as an attack dog.

Gloria Greenfield—Mallory's mom.

Amber DeSilva—Mallory's sister, whom Mallory has never met before.

Conrad Burdock—He's searching for Gloria but wants to find the fabulous blue diamond he suspects she has with her.

Felix Komenda—An artist from Sierra Leone who knows Gloria and raised Amber.

Chapter One

At the base of a seven-hundred-foot granite cliff, Shane Reilly adjusted his sunglasses and stared at the rock climbers from the Aspen/Pitkin County Search and Rescue team as they made their descent. On the way down, they scrutinized every inch, looking for a scrap of material, a blood smear, a hair clip—anything, any trace of the woman who had gone missing four days ago.

To get to this position at the foot of the cliff, Shane had driven down a steep one-lane service road. His assignment was to search this wide flat canyon where a scrawny creek wound through leafless shrubs, scruffy pines, rocks and patches of October snow that glittered like diamonds in the afternoon sunlight. If the missing woman had dared to hike through this desolate terrain, she must have been desperate to make her getaway. If she'd fallen…he was looking for a dead body.

Head tilted back, he studied the jagged rock face and mentally mapped the route he would have taken if he'd been hired by a group for a day of extreme skiing in the areas outside the groomed slopes. A decade ago, when he was still in his teens, Shane loved being dropped by helicopter into uncharted mountain territory and maneuvering his way down. Then he turned pro and had to be more careful. Skiing had been his life. Until the crash.

He lowered his gaze. The rugged territory had already been surveyed by drones. This effort was a more detailed search—the specialty of Shane's partner, Elvis. The seventy-two-pound, black Labrador retriever kept his tail in the air and his nose to the ground, moving purposefully, searching. His sense of smell, which was ten thousand times more effective than a human, alerted him to the presence of skittering voles as well as elk, coyote and mountain lion. *Layers and layers of scent.* Using a T-shirt that belonged to the missing woman, Elvis could track her through an old-growth forest or across the Colorado high plains. With minimal instruction from Shane, the Lab had divided the wide ravine into quadrants as soon as they arrived. So far, Elvis hadn't shown any indication of a find.

"How are you doing?" Shane glanced over his shoulder to his backpack, where he carried a water jug and collapsible bowl for Elvis. All that sniffing could be dehydrating. "Thirsty?"

Without pausing, Elvis chuffed impatiently as if to say, "Hey, I'm working here."

"Yeah, yeah, don't mind me. I'm just the guy who buys that pricey kibble you like."

Shane always talked to his Lab and, frankly, wouldn't have been too shocked if the dog answered back. Elvis had been his best friend since they were introduced at the physical therapy clinic after the skiing accident. The doctors had told Shane he might never walk again, but Elvis—his assigned service dog—never gave up on him.

When Shane strode out the door from rehab, he brought Elvis with him. For the past two years, they'd undergone

SAR training together. Shane had started skiing again. Not professionally, just for fun. And he'd opened his own business. Most of the time, life was good.

Elvis raised his head, went into high alert and shook all over. His feet scrambled in the gravelly dirt, and he bounded toward the cliff face. At the edge of a tall arched boulder, he sat and froze in place, which was his signal for a find.

Shane dashed toward Elvis. Was this the missing woman or something else? If the dog had sensed danger, he would have been in attack mode. This find was probably harmless. Nonetheless, Shane was glad for the Glock 17 in the holster clipped to his belt. He drew his weapon. Couldn't ignore the possibility that the woman who had disappeared might have been kidnapped.

Gun in hand, he stopped beside Elvis. "Heel."

The black Lab stood at his left hip, ready and waiting for the next command from Shane, the alpha of their little pack.

"Whoever is behind that rock, step out," Shane said. "Show me your hands."

The woman who emerged with hands raised had long blond hair cascading past her shoulders almost to her waist. Even though she wore jeans and an oversize flannel shirt, she looked like an angel. *Thank you, Elvis, for finding her.*

Shane peeled off his Ray-Bans and asked, "Who are you?"

"Mallory Greenfield. The person you're looking for is my mother, Gloria."

Though she spoke clearly, he barely made sense of her words. Consumed by inappropriate desire, he yearned to tangle his fingers in those silky blond strands and kiss those full pink lips. *Get a grip, Shaney boy. Been too long since you've had a date.* "Why were you hiding in the rocks?"

"I didn't want to disturb your search. I'm wearing Mom's shirt, and I thought your dog might smell it."

"Which he did." He holstered his Glock. "You can put your hands down."

"Thanks." She jammed her fists into her pockets and frowned.

She was still beautiful, but her unhappiness disturbed him. "What's wrong?"

She glared, and he realized what a dumb question that was. Of course, she was upset. Her mother was missing. "Who wants to know?"

"I'm Shane Reilly." He reached down and patted the Lab. "This is Elvis."

"Why do you call him Elvis?"

"For one thing, he ain't nothing but a hound dog." Shane tried on a disarming grin. "And take a look at his mouth."

She leaned close to study the handsome dog's upper left lip. Elvis the dog mimicked the sexy sneer of his rock star namesake. Mallory looked from the Lab to Shane and back. Then, she gave an enthusiastic laugh that made the world seem brighter. "Does he sing?"

Shane gave a command that wasn't in the regular training manual. "Give us a song. And-a-one-and-a-two-and-a—"

Elvis tilted his head back and yipped.

Mallory applauded. Her scowl was gone. "Can I pet him?"

"He'll be disappointed if you don't."

After a few gentle pats on his round noggin and scratching under his chin, she fondled his floppy ears, then stroked from head to tail. She hugged Elvis, and he gave a happy murmur in the back of his throat. *Some dogs have all the luck.*

Without letting go of her new best friend, she glanced up. "I've heard of you, Shane Reilly. You were a pro skier, competed in the Olympics in downhill and slalom."

"And now, I'm retired."

"What do you do?"

"For one thing, I volunteer with Search and Rescue. Me and Elvis are getting pretty good at SAR." He gazed into her wide-set eyes, which were an incredible shade of turquoise blue. "And I'm a full-time licensed private investigator."

"Really?"

"Elvis was learning how to be a crime solver, and I figured I should do the same. Plus my father and brother are cops in Denver."

"Why didn't you join them?"

"I wanted to have free time for skiing, and you'd be surprised by how many people in Aspen need my services."

She stood, looked him up and down and stuck out her hand. "You're hired, Shane. I want you and Elvis to find my mom."

He grasped her small delicate hand in his and lightly squeezed. "Where do we start?"

"She left a note."

"What did it say?"

She reclaimed her hand and dashed a tear off her cheek. "It said, I'll be back."

Not much to work with, but he'd do anything to find Gloria Greenfield and bring a smile to Mallory's beautiful face.

TWO AND A half days later at the bitter edge of dawn, Mallory turned off her alarm before the buzzer sounded. She'd barely slept. Her mom was still missing. During the past six days, her mood had alternated between elation when a clue arose to panic when she feared Gloria was gone forever, and then to despair and exhaustion. *Where the hell has she gone?*

In thick wool socks, Mallory padded to her bedroom window and threw open the curtains. Snow battered the beveled panes. This marked the first real storm of the season, a cause for celebration in Aspen where the fiscal well-being of the town meant at least twenty-five inches of base and a fresh supply of champagne powder. Mallory's fortunes weren't directly tied to the weather, but her business also depended on tourists and skiers. She was a part owner of Reflections, an art gallery and coffee shop perched at the edge of the cliff where she'd met Shane and Elvis at the bottom. Though Gloria had founded the gallery, she delegated much of the responsibility to Mallory.

For the past several months, Reflections hadn't been doing well. They'd barely survived the COVID shutdown and were still struggling toward recovery, relying mostly on the sale of baked goods, coffee and tea. Though tempted to close the doors and devote herself 24/7 to searching for her mother, Mallory suspected that would be signing a death warrant for Reflections. She couldn't take time off for grief. People depended on her, and the business wasn't going to run itself.

After a quick shower, she plaited her hair into a long braid, tossed on her clothes, shoved her feet into snow boots and donned her parka, hat and gloves. She lived close enough to the gallery that she was able to slog through the knee-high drifts and unlock the rear door. In the mud-room outside the kitchen, she changed from her boots into green slip-resistant clogs, and then she started the early morning prep work—mixing, kneading and proofing the dough for fresh breads and pastries. With muffins and scones in the oven, she took a caffeine break and pushed through the swinging kitchen door into the coffee shop adjoining the gallery.

Sipping her favorite dark roast brew, she peered through a window at the unabated snowfall on the sculpture garden at the edge of the cliff. Was her mother out there, freezing and lost? Suffering from a delusion? Hiding from someone or something that would do her harm? Mallory pinched her lips together to hold back a sob but couldn't stop her tears. *Don't give up.* She had to keep believing that Gloria would come home safe and sound. Living without her was unthinkable.

Given her mom's eccentric and unpredictable nature, her disappearance could be based on a whim or a half-baked scheme. That was Uncle Walter's opinion. Not really a relative, Walter Pulaski had been in Mallory's life for as long as she could remember. Not only was he internationally known as a sculptor who worked primarily in marble from a local quarry, but he also provided Mallory with grandfatherly guidance, ranging from bedtime fables to advice on creating wood carvings of forest creatures and totem poles. The end products were inexpensive and sold well. Not that Mallory considered whittling to be a viable career.

Walter hadn't known where Gloria went. Nor had any of her other friends, employees or ex-boyfriends. Everyone had said, "You know Gloria. She'll turn up."

Mallory wasn't so sure.

She glanced down at her cell phone. *Call Shane.* She'd begun to look forward to their frequent talks and seeing the singing dog with the Elvis sneer. Right now, she wanted reassurance, needed to talk to a kind-hearted, understanding person. She flashed on a mental picture of Shane, who was big—about six feet two inches—and comforting. His sun-streaked brown hair fell across his tanned forehead. He had stubble on his chin. When he grinned, dimples bracketed his mouth. *Call him.* It was after seven o'clock, not too early.

She tapped his number on speed dial, and he answered immediately in a clear, wide-awake voice. "Are you at work?"

"Where else would I be at dawn?"

"You might find this strange, but there are people who actually sleep until eight. Sometimes even later."

"Mom always says there's plenty of time to rest when you're dead." *Not dead, oh, please, not dead.* Another spurt of tears spilled down her cheeks. "This weather has me worried."

"I understand," he said. "You're right to worry. But I got to tell you, I love snow."

Of course, he did. He used to be a pro skier. Before they'd officially met, she'd seen him on the slopes and admired his form. He looked good on skis and even better close up. His hair was perpetually rumpled but not messy. Thick black lashes circled his caramel-brown eyes. Thinking of him gave her a much-needed distraction. "Can you come over today?"

"How about now? I bet you've got fresh muffins in the oven."

"Now is fine." Better than she'd hoped for, but she didn't want to come right out and tell him that she was smitten. There were already enough complications to deal with. "And why are you awake at this ungodly hour?"

"Doing cyber research on your mom. It's two hours later in NYC."

"Why are you researching New York?"

"An art connection to your gallery. I'm always working. A great PI never sleeps." He paused for effect. "Just ask Elvis."

At the sound of his name, the Lab gave a bark.

Shane responded, "That's right, isn't it? You're a great detective."

Mallory imagined the dog spinning in a circle, chasing his tail and wiggling his hindquarters. "Be sure to bring him along."

"You hear that, buddy? She can't help falling in love with you."

She groaned at the song reference. "Come to the kitchen door. It's unlocked."

As soon as she disconnected the call, she stared at the silent phone and wished she'd hear from her mom. The only texts she'd gotten this morning were from employees who would be late. On a typical weekday, at least one of the bakers would have shown up by now. Not that she needed help. The gallery and coffee shop didn't open until ten o'clock, and the monster snowfall would keep people away. Despite the need for paying customers, she hoped for a quiet day. No sooner had that thought registered in her brain than she heard loud thuds. Someone was pounding on the hand-carved doors at the entrance. A woman called out, demanding to be let in.

Mallory pocketed her phone, got to her feet and clomped across the gray-and-brown travertine tiles that reminded her of river rocks. She patted her cheeks, erasing every trace of moisture. Why had this person—this woman—come here? Did she have something to do with Gloria? *Oh, God, I hope so.* About time she'd catch a break.

The voice shouted, "It's cold. Let me in."

Mallory unfastened the dead bolt, unlocked the door and opened it. Outside, partially sheltered from the heavy snowfall by an overhanging eave, stood a tall woman in a black parka. A fur-trimmed hood hid her face.

She shoved against the door and stormed inside. "Thank God, I got here in time. He intends to kill you."

Chapter Two

After nearly a week of fear and confusion, Mallory didn't think she could be taken off guard, but this strange woman had hit her with an unexpected gut shot. Off-balance, Mallory staggered backward a step and bumped into an easel advertising the showing next week for the kindergarten through to fourth-grade classes she taught in the afternoon. She caught the poster before it fell and turned to the stranger. "Who wants to kill me?"

"Conrad Burdock. Actually, he's looking for your mother." The way her voice dropped when she said *mother* made the word sound like a curse.

Nascent hope shot through Mallory. Maybe something could be gained from this bizarre encounter. "What do you know about Gloria?"

"Quite a lot, actually. I'll tell you later. Right now, we've got to run, Mallory."

How does she know my name? "I've never heard of this Burdock."

"I'm trying to tell you. Don't be so stupid." The tall woman slammed the heavy door with a crash that echoed all the way up to the open beam ceiling. She adjusted the shoulder strap on a large leather messenger bag and focused on Mallory. "Listen to me. Do as I say and maybe, just maybe, you'll survive."

"Tell me what you know about my mom."

"First," the woman said, "you come with me."

"Into the blizzard?"

"Unless you can sprout wings and fly."

Now who is being stupid? Mallory pointed to her froggy green clogs. "I'm not dressed to tromp through the snow. If I agree to go outside with you, I have to change into my coat and boots. They're in the kitchen."

"Is anybody else in the kitchen?"

"I'm here alone. And I have muffins in the oven." When the woman unzipped her parka and pulled off her gloves, Mallory's gaze riveted to a gun holster clipped to her belt. The intruder's rude attitude took on a more sinister aspect, and she was grateful that Shane and Elvis would be here at any moment. She decided to stall until her backup arrived. "I want more information, okay?"

"We don't have time to play around. Get your damn boots."

Mallory had grown up dealing with difficult artists and angry customers and various other people her mom rubbed the wrong way. Her tone of voice took on a soothing tone, and she arranged her features in a conciliatory expression. She led the way along the carved half wall that separated the coffee shop from the gallery itself. "Back here, through the swinging doors."

"Nice place you've got here. Lots of polished wood and excellent sculptures."

"By Pulaski." Even under threat, Mallory couldn't help bragging about Uncle Walter.

"Walter Pulaski? I'm impressed."

"Reflections used to be a restaurant. All open space with the kitchen in the rear. Setting up the partitions and the lecture area took some work, but the end result was worth it." Over her shoulder, she said, "Doesn't seem fair. You know my name, but I don't know yours."

"Amber DeSilva."

"Like the gem?"

"Amber is a fossilized resin, not a gemstone." Though her voice oozed disdain, she stopped short of accusing Mallory of stupidity, again. "Don't you know me?"

Was she supposed to recognize this person? "Sorry."

At the kitchen door, she caught Mallory's arm and turned her around so they were face-to-face. "Look at my face. My eyes."

The color of her chin-length blond hair nearly matched Mallory's long braid. The symmetry of their features—upturned nose, wide mouth, square jaw—was similar. When Mallory gazed deeply into Amber's eyes, the green-blue color of her irises astonished her. An exact match to Mallory, but that was impossible. Nobody else had eyes like hers, nobody except her mom. The most notable difference between them was height. Mallory stood five feet four inches, and Amber had to be nearly six feet tall in her high-heeled boots.

Cautiously, Mallory admitted, "I see a resemblance."

Amber gave a snort. "Ya think?"

"Let's have a cup of coffee before we rush into anything." When she pushed open the kitchen door, the comforting aroma of baking breads and muffins wafted over them. "I really don't want to go outside again. It's freezing."

"You're not listening, damn it." Amber followed her

into the huge kitchen. "This is a matter of life and death. We have to find your mother before Burdock gets here."

"We're on the same page. I'm really worried about her and want to find her. Have you heard anything? Do you know where she is?"

Amber gave a short harsh laugh. "She didn't tell you that she was leaving, did she? Whisked away like magic. She's the queen of hocus-pocus. Ha! Doesn't feel nice to be left behind, does it?"

What was she talking about? "How well do you know my mom?"

"Oh, my God, you still don't get it. Look at me again. Look close."

Mallory took another glance and then shrugged. "Sorry."

Amber DeSilva framed Mallory's face between her hands and stared with her turquoise eyes. "Mallory, my love, I'm your sister."

Stunned, Mallory gaped. *Her sister?* Not possible! According to Gloria, her father died before Mallory was born, and they had no other living relations on either side. Either Amber had fabricated a weird, complicated lie or Gloria had a whole different life before she met Mallory's father. Conceivably she'd been married before and had other children. But why hadn't she mentioned another family?

"You must mean that you're my half sister." Mallory leaned forward, trying to get closer to the truth. "From an earlier marriage."

"Wrong! We have the same father, Raymond DeSilva, and the same mother, Ingrid DeSilva, who you call Gloria Greenfield. You know, I'd love to sit down for a sweet little chat with tea and crumpets, but we damn well don't have time. Get your buns out of the oven and put on your boots."

"How long have you known about me?"

"Only a few days. Once I had the name you were using, tracking you down was easy."

"I don't have a fake name."

Amber gave her a smug grin. "I'm sure Gloria filed all the fake paperwork. She spared no expense, stole enough to get the two of you started on a lovely new life. How sweet. How lovely. How selfish."

"How old are you?"

"I'm four years older than you."

My big sister. A strange feeling—a jumbled combination of joy and fear, happiness and dread—surged through her. She wasn't alone anymore. And her life was completely different.

MOST OF THE mountain roads and streets hadn't been cleared, but Shane drove his Lincoln Navigator SUV, a deluxe 4WD gift from a former sponsor, through the steadily falling snow with no skids, no slips, no problems. The full force of the storm was subsiding, and he guessed they'd get only eight to ten inches—significant but not crippling for Aspen.

In the rear of the SUV, Elvis rode in his specially designed pen where he could watch the snow from windows on both sides. He'd already been out this morning and raced around the fenced area behind Shane's cabin, tunneled into high drifts and buried himself under the glorious snowfall. Before Mallory called, Shane had taken the time to rub dry the dog's shiny black coat. Elvis still smelled doggy, but Shane didn't notice anymore. The Lab was his best friend, and it seemed rude to complain about his natural odor.

In the rearview mirror, Shane saw Elvis staring toward the front of the Navigator. His pink tongue lolled from one side of his mouth while the other side smirked. "We're going to see Mallory. You like her, right?"

A happy bark followed a shoulder shimmy.

"You understand, though, she's more my type than yours."

Elvis growled. He wasn't buying that logic.

"We could find a lady friend for you. Maybe a French poodle."

"Yip. Yip. Yip."

"Okay, three French poodles."

The Navigator rounded a final curve where snowplows had scraped off the parking lot in front of a strip mall and gas station. The art gallery came into view. Lights were on. A glow came from the north-facing windows nearest the entrance. The soaring eaves of Reflections resembled the bow of a clipper ship churning through the snowstorm toward the edge of a treacherous cliff that had claimed the lives of at least five rock climbers. A thick layer of snow piled on the slanted roof and on dozens of heavy marble sculptures in the garden.

Shane had visited plenty of museums and elite galleries around the world while on ski tours, and Reflections impressed him. Mallory's mom had done an outstanding job redesigning this structure, curating the displays and building a reputation. From what he'd heard, artists competed aggressively to be granted a showing here in Aspen, where ski bums rubbed elbows with rich and famous mountain residents.

He frowned to himself. Mallory wasn't going to like the information he'd unearthed in his latest online research. Much of his investigating happened on the computer, and he was skilled at navigating the ins and outs. Gloria Greenfield—art gallery owner and boho-chic free spirit—kept a relatively low-profile on social media with very few photographs. A cause for him to wonder what she was hiding.

Her life before Mallory's birth twenty-six years ago was sketchy. Her hometown in Texas had no records of her. The high school didn't have a photo of her in the yearbook, and the same held true for the art school she attended. Granted, computer data from that era wasn't always efficient or reliable, but he'd expected to fill in some of the blanks. The more questions he'd uncovered about her background, the more Gloria's disappearance smelled like something illegal and dangerous.

Outside Reflections, he saw an SUV parked near the front entrance. It seemed out of place. Shane doubted that the vehicle belonged to an employee. They usually entered through the kitchen where they could hang their coats and scarves in the mudroom before getting started. Tire tracks were still visible in the parking lot, indicating that the SUV hadn't been there for long. Too early for a customer or a friendly visit.

Shane followed a road at the edge of the parking lot and drove around to the rear where he parked. Mallory's car wasn't there, which was no big surprise because she often walked to work. He unlocked the compartment under the center console, removed his Glock 17, checked the clip and slipped the weapon into a belt holster. Not knowing what to expect, he needed to be prepared for anything.

Before entering through the kitchen door, he glanced down at Elvis. In spite of the Lab's high spirits, he was obedient. "Elvis, heel."

Instantly, the dog transformed into a SAR professional, sitting at Shane's side and waiting for further instruction. Shane placed his index finger across his lips. "Elvis, hush."

Confident that the Lab wouldn't make a sound, Shane entered the mudroom, shucked off his parka and drew his gun. *Ready for action.* Hearing voices from the kitchen at the back of the restaurant, he crept closer to the door that separated the mudroom from the kitchen, pushed it slightly open and listened. Elvis sat beside him, silent and alert.

The voice of a stranger said, "Your coffee smells good."

"I can make you a travel mug." That was Mallory.

"We don't have time. Besides, I don't expect your mountain coffee to be anywhere as delicious as my special brew in New York."

"This is an Ethiopian blend, fair trade and dark roasted."

"Don't care," said the stranger. "Hurry up and don't try anything cute. I don't want to hurt you, but you should know that I'm an excellent markswoman. Learned to shoot in Sierra Leone."

"Didn't you say just say you're from New York?"

"I often visited Africa with my father. He was a gemologist."

In his cyber research, Shane had learned that Gloria sold precious gems several years ago. A possible connection with this stranger from Africa. He recalled what he knew of conflict diamonds, also called blood diamonds, which were used to finance insurgents and warlords.

"I'm not going anywhere with you." Mallory's tone rang with determination. "Even if we are sisters…"

Shane swallowed his surprise. *Sisters?*

Mallory continued, "Why should I believe what you say? Why would some guy I've never heard of want to find Gloria and kill her?"

"Oh, my sweet, stupid Mallory. He doesn't care about Gloria or about you. Burdock is after the African Teardrop."

"What?" she gasped. "What do you know about the Teardrop?"

Supremely confident, the stranger continued, "A 521-carat, pale blue diamond that went missing at just about the same time my mother, Ingrid DeSilva, was killed in an explosion."

"What are you saying?"

"My mother—sorry, I guess that's *our* mother—faked her own death, disappeared and stole a small fortune in gems from *our* father, including the Teardrop. She couldn't sell or fence that particular diamond because it was too famous. Does any of this sound familiar?"

"Mom said the Teardrop was cursed."

"Well, she might be right about that. Conrad Burdock has already killed people in his search for that stone. He'll kill again."

Shane had heard enough. He stepped into the kitchen with his Glock braced in both hands. "Don't move."

Beside him, Elvis bared his teeth and growled.

When the tall blonde reached for her holster, Shane snapped, "Don't try it. Raise your hands over your head. Do it."

Though this wasn't the first time he'd faced off with a dangerous adversary, Shane did most of his sleuthing online or by interviewing witnesses. He'd taken training courses to get his license, and his brother, the Denver cop, had given him lessons on how to apprehend and subdue, but he was uncomfortable threatening a woman, especially a woman who looked enough like Mallory to be her actual sister. Still, he kept his Glock aimed in her direction as she lifted her hands over her head.

"It's okay," Mallory said. "She's not here to hurt me."

"Then she won't mind if you disarm her." He nodded toward the woman. "Take her weapon."

"Honestly, Shane. You're overreacting." Still, Mallory followed his instruction and approached the woman. "I'm sorry, Amber. I need to do what he says."

"Who the hell is he?"

Mallory unfastened the safety strap on the holster and carefully removed the Beretta. "His name is Shane Reilly, and he's a private investigator I hired to find Mom. Shane, this is Amber DeSilva, and she claims to be my sister."

"You never mentioned a sister."

"Because I didn't know about her," Mallory said.

Amber exhaled a frustrated groan and pointed toward her leather messenger bag. "I brought a laptop with me. You can look me up."

That would have been Shane's next move. Computer research didn't count as an infallible source for verification, but it gave something to start with. "Okay, sis. Are you carrying any other weapons?"

"I'm not. Trust me?"

"No."

She cocked an eyebrow. "Then I guess you'll just have to do a full body search."

If Mallory had issued that invite, he would have responded in a flash. He'd been longing to slide his hands over her body from the first moment he saw her, but she hadn't given him the okay signal.

"Quit fussing at each other," Mallory said. "Listen carefully, Shane, because I'm not going to repeat this."

She repeated the unbelievable story about Gloria stealing a fabulous gemstone and faking her death during the Civil War in Sierra Leone. He knew her Mom was eccentric, but this was over the top.

"Come on," Amber urged. "We need to hurry."

"Why?"

"I was careful to make sure Burdock's men didn't follow me from the airport, but they're smart enough to figure out the address of this place. It's not safe to stay here."

Or maybe she led these supposed bad guys directly here. Or maybe they didn't exist. He hadn't seen another vehicle out front. Shane lowered his weapon but didn't slide it into the belt holster.

"I should go," Mallory said. "If we don't, she's going to keep harping on it."

"Damn right, I am."

When Amber glared, Shane noticed the unusual turquoise color of her eyes—another indication of a sibling relationship with Mallory. Her story was bizarre, but it might be true. He had questions for her.

Amber dropped her hands and concentrated all her attention on her alleged sister. "This is important, Mallory. Do you know where the Teardrop is?"

"I only saw it once. I was probably ten and didn't realize it was real or valuable." Mallory ducked into the mudroom. "Let me change into my boots. If we hurry, we can get this figured out and be back here by opening time at ten."

"I'll drive," Shane said. "My car is more comfortable for Elvis."

"I'm guessing Elvis is your dog." Amber sneered. "Cute."

Hearing his name, the Lab perked up. But he didn't bounce over toward the tall blonde or even wag his tail. Apparently, Elvis didn't trust Amber, either.

Mallory emerged from the back room wearing her boots and parka. She carried ski gloves in her hands. "Let me lock the front door, and we can get going."

Shane heard the heavy front door crash open. Then came a shout. And the clatter of boots on tile.

Chapter Three

Amber's dire warning had come true. Or had it?

Was this a setup? Shane glanced past Mallory, who stood frozen in the middle of the kitchen and concentrated on Amber. Her haughty expression succumbed to panic. Tension and fear distorted her features. Amber was damn scared, and the people who'd charged through the front door had to be the ones who frightened her. Shane still didn't trust her motives, but he believed her terror was real.

They needed to move fast, before the intruders figured out that they were in the kitchen. While he kept his Glock trained on the swinging door from the gallery, Shane herded the women and Elvis toward the rear door. "Get in my car."

"Key fob?" Mallory held out her hand.

"It's unlocked."

"What if I want to start the engine?"

He handed over the fob. "I'll drive. Wait for me."

As soon as the women disappeared into the mudroom, he braced himself. For a brief moment, he considered stepping into the gallery and attempting to work out some kind of compromise, but the continued shouts and crashes indicated violent intent. These guys hadn't come here for a negotiation. This was a hostile assault.

The door from the gallery swung wide. Two men wearing black ski masks and heavy parkas charged into the kitchen. In a quick scan, they spotted Shane. Handguns raised, they aimed and fired. Four shots. Four misses.

He raised his Glock and returned fire. The taller guy yelped and fell to the floor.

Before his brain had time to process the fact that he might have killed a man, Shane pivoted and dove through the door into the mudroom. Grabbing his parka, he dashed outside.

Mallory hadn't waited for him to take the driver's seat. She sat behind the steering wheel with the windshield cleared and the engine running. *Smart move. He couldn't complain.*

He jumped into the passenger side. "Go."

Even though she wasn't familiar with Shane's 4WD Lincoln, she deftly maneuvered out from behind Reflections before one of the intruders burst through the back door and started firing at them. Bullets thudded against the rear of his car. In the back seat, Amber whimpered and wrapped her arms around Elvis, who had apparently forgotten that he didn't like this woman. He buried his nose in the fur-trimmed collar of her parka.

Looking over his shoulder, Shane saw the boxy outline of a Hummer crossing the parking lot and stopping at the rear door. How many of them were there? He'd seen two in the kitchen, including the guy who'd fallen, and a third must be driving the tank-like vehicle. Were there others? His Glock handgun didn't seem like enough defense. He asked Amber, "Did you pick up your Beretta?"

Her eyes were wide and frightened. "I have my gun."

"And you know how to use it, right?"

She swallowed hard. "I'm not a good shot from a moving vehicle."

"Nobody is," he said. "We might need the fire power later."

"I'll be ready."

Her trembling voice sounded anything but ready for a shoot-out. Oddly enough, Mallory—who appeared to be a peace-loving flower child—was the coolest person in their little combat group. She drove like a champ, skidding at the edge of disaster but not going too far. Her gloved hands rested steady on the wheel. When the Navigator reached the stop sign at the street that had been cleared earlier this morning, she executed a sharp left turn without slowing. Dangerous move but nobody else was on the road. They were headed into town.

Shane took his phone from his pocket. "Drive directly to police headquarters. I'll call ahead and let them know we're coming."

"No."

"Did you say no? You won't go to the police station?"

"Yes, I said no."

Her flat refusal didn't make sense. Mallory had worked with the sheriff and the police chief during the search for her mother, which meant she didn't have a built-in resentment against law enforcement in general. He kept his tone level and calm, which wasn't the way he felt. Shane was, after all, the son of a cop. "When somebody shoots at you, it's wise to tell the police. At least, let me call."

"No." She was more adamant.

From the back seat, Amber called out, "I see headlights following us."

If the thugs who attacked at Reflections were on their

tail, they had even more reason to contact the authorities. But Mallory had a different idea. At the next snowplowed road, she took a right and raced past four other cross streets to a stoplight. Through the thick veil of falling snow, he spotted the headlights behind them. At this distance, he couldn't tell if the other vehicle was a Hummer or not. "Why won't you go to the police?"

"Because I love my mother. I'll do anything for her."

"You care about Gloria. I get that." The bond with her mother ran deep and true. "But what does that have to do with police protection?"

"If half of what Amber told me is true, my mother broke the law. She faked her death and stole a fortune in precious gems. If we contact the police, there will be investigations and prosecutions. I refuse to be the person who sends Mom to jail."

She cranked the steering wheel and turned left again. Too fast. The back of the car fishtailed wildly. The moment she got the skid under control, she went left again, then drove back to the main road. She checked her rearview mirror. "Did we lose them?"

In the back seat, Amber and Elvis stared through the rear window. "I can't tell," Amber said. "There are a couple of other cars."

"We might be able to end this right away," Mallory said. "We're going to Mom's place. I remember where she hid the Teardrop after she showed it to me. Maybe it's still there."

"Not likely," Amber said. "Wasn't that several years ago?"

"Sixteen years. It's still possible."

Shane had no comment. Gloria's A-frame house had been their first stop when he signed on to be Mallory's PI.

Together, they'd searched for clues in her desk drawers, her closets, her bedside table and even her pantry. He'd learned quite a bit about her mother but nothing that pointed to her location. And he remembered the final stretch leading to the house. The road bordered a rugged granite wall on the left. The other side was a drop of a couple hundred feet. Not the sort of road to be driving on in a storm, especially not with bad guys on their tail. "This might not be the best time," he said.

"Can't hurt to try."

He knew she wouldn't be dissuaded. Mallory could be as sweet as a baby fawn but had the tenacity of a badger when she made up her mind. In that respect, she was somewhat like Gloria. The only way he could keep her safe was if he had control of the situation. Never again would he agree for her to be the one behind the wheel.

She dodged through a couple more changes of direction and circled around until she and Amber felt sure they'd lost the Hummer. Mallory set her course for her mother's A-frame house in a high canyon.

While the morning sunlight fought a losing battle with overcast skies, he peered in the direction of the ski runs on Aspen Mountain, which were obscured by a curtain of falling snow. The chair lifts and gondolas weren't open yet, but in a few short weeks, the slopes would be filled with skiers and snowboarders. Every year since he'd turned eighteen and moved to Aspen full-time, he'd looked forward to opening day. This season, he hoped Mallory would be with him, flying downhill and soaring over moguls. He wanted to hear her laughter ringing in the frosty air, to see the roses in her cheeks and the sparkle in her turquoise eyes.

She guided his Navigator into the series of winding turns that led to Gloria's house. When they entered the stretch with the steep drop on the passenger side, he held his breath and slammed his foot down on the floorboard to press an invisible brake. A treacherous ride but no one appeared to be chasing them.

Covered in several inches of snow, the odd-shaped house—partly A-frame with a couple of gables and a wall of glass on one side—reminded him of a fairy-tale dwelling. A place where elves and fairies might live. He told Mallory not to park in the driveway where they might get stuck in the snow. "We don't want anybody to pull in behind us and block our way out."

He swiveled his head and looked at Amber in the back seat. "Have you disabled your cell phone so your location can't be traced?"

"How would I do that?"

Inwardly, he groaned. Amber acted like she was tough and worldly-wise. A lot of bluster, but she had very little idea of what it took to be on the run, evading the alleged villain. What was his name? Conrad something? "Give me the phone."

"You're not going to erase my contacts or anything, are you?"

There were several apps to block locators, but he opted for the quick-and-easy method. "I'm turning it off and taking out your battery. When you need to make a call, let me know."

Mallory parked uphill, off the side of the unplowed road. Though their tracks through the snow couldn't be hidden or erased, their position was set for a quick escape.

Shane held out his hand for the fob. "You did good."

"I was born and raised in the mountains. I know how to drive through snow."

He took a moment to fasten his dog's flashy red leather harness with shiny studs. A little bit sexy and a little bit rock 'n' roll, it was perfect for a Lab named Elvis. Shane didn't hook the leash onto the harness, preferring to let Elvis bound ahead while they slogged through the snow to the rear door.

"The dog shouldn't be with us," Amber said. "He'll make noise."

"That's the point." Mallory kicked through snow that came almost to her knees. "He'll alert us to anybody approaching."

Shane didn't need a doggy alert to the danger he suspected wasn't far from them, but he liked having the seventy-two-pound black Labrador on his side in a fight. In addition to training as an attack dog, Elvis had killer instincts and a ferocious growl.

Reaching inside his parka, Shane rested his gloved hand on the butt of his holstered Glock while Mallory used her key to unlock the back door. She entered an open kitchen that was separated from a long dining room table by a counter where a collection of mushrooms—porcelain, wood and clay—were displayed. Doodads and tchotchkes filled every space in a design scheme that could only be described as chaotic but not unpleasant. He liked the house and wanted to meet the woman who lived there. A cozy warmth snuggled around him. The many windows on two sides of the kitchen, which must have been added on to the original structure, made him feel like they'd entered a snow globe.

"It's weird," Mallory said, "to be coming in here without hearing Mom's music. The greatest hits of the '90s."

"I remember." Amber's tone was uncharacteristically pleasant. "Lots of Madonna and Michael Jackson. She loved to dance the 'Macarena.'"

For the first time, Shane sensed that Amber's connection with Mallory might be the truth. Her unexpected appearance at Reflections had seemed too coincidental. And her story about a multi-million-dollar stolen diamond sounded like a fantasy. In spite of their matching turquoise irises, Amber had no proof that they were sisters.

"Watch me now." Mallory skipped into the front room in front of the long dining table. Humming tunelessly, she moved in a horizontal line, clapped her hands and returned in the opposite direction.

Elvis tried to match her steps, but it was Amber who faced her and provided a mirror image. At the end of the line, she said the magic words. "Can't touch this."

They went the other way. Together, they repeated the MC Hammer line. "Can't touch this."

Mallory laughed. "Did Mom teach you this dance?"

"Actually, it was Felix." She whirled, and her parka opened wide, revealing her belt holster with the Beretta tucked inside.

"Who's Felix?" Shane asked.

"A friend from Sierra Leone. He came home with Dad after my mother was supposedly killed in an explosion in Freetown. Their two-story office building burned for over forty-eight hours. Everything was incinerated. Most of the inventory of gems were lost."

"I didn't think diamonds could burn," Mallory said.

Amber stopped dancing. Her voice took on a smug,

superior tone as she explained, "Diamonds are made of carbon, like coal. So, yes, they can burn at extreme heat. Dad found a few intact. But the insurance paid for most of his loss."

Shane had another question. "Why didn't he keep the inventory in a fireproof safe?"

"He did," she said coldly. "The door to the safe was opened. Investigators believed that my mother opened it in the hope that she could rescue the gems, but she couldn't escape before the fire overwhelmed her. Before you ask, there was evidence of human remains but no way of identifying the victim. So long ago in a war zone, DNA testing couldn't be counted on. In the back of the safe, they found her wedding ring."

Mallory shuddered. "I know the story is untrue. Mom survived, and so did I. But it must have been horrible for you."

"It was." She flicked her wrist as if she could dismiss a lifetime of bad memories. "Felix helped. I was the only four-year-old in Manhattan with an extremely tall male nanny from Sierra Leone with tattoos up and down both arms. He told me all kinds of good stories about my mother. But I didn't believe a word."

"Why not?" Mallory gazed at her with deep sympathy.

"If my mother was such a wonderful person, why did she abandon me?"

Shane watched and cringed. If these two were, in fact, sisters, the differences between them made a stark contrast. A walking illustration of nature versus nurture, they shared genetics but had been brought up differently, and they wanted very different things. Heartbroken, Mallory desperately yearned to find and protect her beloved mother who had been the center of her life since birth. Amber couldn't care less about Gloria. She was after a big payoff from the sale of the Teardrop and figured her mother owed her that much.

Mallory sighed. "I wish you could know her the way I do."

"Back at you," Amber said. "If you knew what she was really like, you might be glad she's gone."

"She'll come back. I just know she will."

"Don't be so sure. She might be—"

"Okay." Shane stepped between them to interrupt that thought. The possibility of her mom's death was already driving Mallory up a wall. "I think you ladies agree on a specific goal. You both want to find the diamond. And that means finding Gloria."

"Yes," Mallory said.

"An uneasy alliance," her sister chimed in.

"Let's get to it," Shane said. "Mallory, you said there was a hiding place somewhere in this house. Where is it?"

Returning to the kitchen, she peeled off her parka and got down on her hands and knees. Though her jeans weren't formfitting, her cute round bottom stuck up in the air, wiggling and distracting him. The more time he spent with her, the more common these moments of instant attraction became. Someday, he might be able to act on these urges. In the meantime, Elvis played surrogate for him, snuggling against Mallory, licking her face and bumping his hindquarters with hers.

In the back of a lower kitchen cabinet, she flipped a small latch and removed a fake wood wall to reveal a safe hidden behind mixing bowls and pans. "The combination is my birthday. I know because Gloria used it for everything."

The lock opened easily, and Shane wondered if this somewhat invisible but easily accessible spot was a good hiding place for a priceless asset. After fishing around in the opening, Mallory pulled out a small, square polished wooden box with dovetailed sides. "The Teardrop was in here. At least, I think so. It was such a long time ago. I might not be remembering correctly."

Amber snatched the box from her hand and tore off the lid. "There's nothing in here, not a thing. Damn, it was too much to hope we'd find it so quickly."

When she discarded the box on the floor, Mallory snatched it up. Sitting cross-legged on the kitchen floor, she probed the satin lining of the box, trying to find a clue or a note. A shred of evidence.

"Forget it," Amber snapped. "Your mother must have realized this was a lame hiding place and moved the diamond."

"You're wrong." Mallory peeled back the velvet on the bottom of the box. She smiled widely. "I knew there was a reason for coming here, a reason for searching."

"What?"

Mallory held up the small object she'd found in the bottom of the box. "A key."

Chapter Four

Mallory held the flat silver key by the cloverleaf top and ran her finger along the teeth on both sides. No logos or other markings, nothing except a six-digit number, which gave no indication of where the key might fit. "A safe-deposit box?"

"We can track that down," Shane said. "Where did Gloria bank?"

"She had personal and business accounts. A local bank where she got wire deposits and another in Denver." She paused and thought. "Oh, and I think there was something in New York that she opened on vacation. I've heard her talk about offshore banking, but that's probably not where she'd have a safe-deposit box. We should check with Uncle Walter. He knows more about her financials than I do."

Before she had finished speaking, Shane stopped paying attention. Elvis tugged at his sleeve and pulled him out of the kitchen toward the front windows of the A-frame section of the house. The interaction between man and dog reminded her of reruns from an old television show about Lassie, a collie with almost telepathic powers of communication. Under her breath, she mumbled the classic line, "What is it, boy? Did Timmy fall down the well?"

Shane rushed back to the kitchen. "We've got to go."

"What's wrong?" Mallory asked.

"The bad guys are here."

She joined him at the window. "Where?"

He patted the black Lab, who was positively vibrating with warning. "Elvis told me."

"Really?" Amber rolled her eyes. "Are we taking orders from the dog?"

"Stay here if you want," Shane said.

He picked up Mallory's parka and dragged her toward the back door. In seconds, they were outside, threading their way through snow-covered lodgepole pines and aspens toward where she'd parked his 4WD Navigator. A layer of snow had already accumulated on the car. With the sleeve of his parka, Shane wiped the driver's side window and the windshield. He got behind the steering wheel while she opened the back for Elvis and ducked into the passenger seat. Using the fob he'd taken from her when they arrived, he fired up the engine.

"Wait," Mallory said. "Amber isn't here."

"Her decision. And who knows? Maybe it's part of her plan. It's possible she's working with Conrad. The thugs in ski masks might answer to her."

"No way. Didn't you see how scared she was?"

"I don't trust your supposed sister," he said, "and I wasn't hired to protect her."

Before he could pull onto the road, Amber threw herself against the back door and leaped inside. "They're almost here. Coming up the front sidewalk."

Shane smoothly accelerated. "So Elvis was right."

"Yeah, yeah, your dog is brilliant." He reached into a pocket of his parka and took out a plastic sandwich bag.

"These are bacon treats. He loves them so don't be stingy, but don't give him all of them."

Around a curve about a hundred yards away, Mallory saw the Hummer that had chased them from Reflections. One man in a black ski mask limped behind the heavy-duty vehicle. He raised his handgun and aimed at them, but Shane was driving too fast for him to take the shot before they zoomed past. Still, he fired at their car as they sped down the road.

When a bullet thumped against the back, Shane winced. She knew how much he liked the Navigator, and the poor thing was taking a beating today. He swooped onto the treacherous part of the route, skirting the perilous drop on the driver's side. He asked, "How do I get to Uncle Walter's place from here?"

"At the bottom of the hill, you'll hit Meadow Ridge. Take a left." Directions to Uncle Walter's lavish château, part of an elite gated community, weren't complicated. She pulled her phone from a pocket and bypassed the apps Shane had installed a few days ago to disguise her signal. "I'll call ahead and let him know we're coming."

Consulting with Walter Pulaski felt like the smart thing to do. If anyone knew about Mom's secret identity, it had to be him. When she'd gone missing, he claimed ignorance regarding her whereabouts, but he confided in Mallory that Gloria—his long-time partner at Reflections—was troubled about the future of the art gallery and told him she had something of great value to sell. The African Teardrop?

She kept her phone conversation with him short, not wanting to give away too much before they talked face-to-face. She needed for him to look her in the eye and be completely honest even if he thought she'd be hurt. Also, she wanted Shane to be there. Not only was he good at asking questions that didn't occur to her—like knowing whether they should trust Amber—but he had investigative skills. He knew about internet searching, interrogations and legal issues.

Glancing across the console at his profile, she noted the sharp edges of his cheekbones, his stubborn jaw and cleft chin. Apart from the dimples at the corners of his mouth that appeared when he smiled, his features were chiseled and hard, almost obstinate. Not unlike his insistence on calling the police. No doubt, that was the right thing to do, and if any other person had disappeared, Mallory wouldn't have hesitated. But this was Gloria! She couldn't betray the woman who birthed and raised her.

While she directed him around the business area of town and into the hills, she made another call and talked to the guard outside Uncle Walter's gated community, warning him that she might be followed by men in ski masks driving a dark-colored Hummer.

"Don't you worry," he said. "I won't let anybody in who doesn't belong."

"Thanks, Henry. And I'd appreciate if you don't mention this to anybody, especially not the authorities."

"Just like your mama." He chuckled. "Don't worry, Mal. Your secrets are safe with me."

As soon as she ended the call, Shane asked, "Why are you dragging this guy in?"

"Into what?"

"Aiding and abetting," he said. "Sooner or later, we have to talk to the police."

From the back seat, Amber groaned. "For a private eye, you're not very adventurous. Why so law-abiding?"

Mallory answered for him, "His father and brother are both cops."

"Well, that explains it."

"Explains nothing," Shane said. "My goal is survival. The odds are better if we have the law on our side."

"Begging to differ," Amber said. "We're talking about a diamond worth twenty million, which opens a lot of doors to bribery. What makes you think the cops would help you?"

Mallory had to agree. Amber had a point—but could she be trusted?

The Navigator approached the tall wrought iron gates at the entrance to Wind Shadow, an exclusive area so high they could look down on everybody else. Mallory saw the road had already been cleared. Henry, the gatekeeper, sat atop a snowplow the size of a Zamboni blocking the way inside.

Mallory jumped out of the SUV and waved.

Henry responded and pulled the snowplow out of the way. As soon as Shane drove through, the obstacle returned to stop any unwanted guests from entering. Mallory waved again and shouted, "You're the best, Henry."

"No problem, cookie. Good luck finding Gloria."

In spite of his encouraging words, he sadly shook his head, which made her think the worst. Mallory responded with defiance, "She'll be back with a story to tell us all."

"That's the spirit."

She directed Shane past several spectacular homes to the swooping, curved driveway, scraped clean of snow, that led to Uncle Walter's stone and cedar chalet. His sculpture studio—the size of a barn with a huge door for transporting massive statues in and out—stood beside his three-car garage. Outside the front door was a massive marble sculpture of a woman in flowing robes and long hair spilling down her back while she reached toward the sky with an outstretched hand that could cradle the stars and moon. Her laughing face bore a remarkable resemblance to Gloria.

Shane parked in the driveway in front of the garage and turned to her. "You and Amber go on inside. Elvis and I will check the damage to my vehicle before we come in."

"Are you sure?"

"Elvis could use a break." The corner of his mouth lifted in a smile, activating his dimples. "And so could I. It's been a fraught morning, and it's not even nine o'clock."

His comment reminded her that she needed to put in a call to Sylvia who usually opened the coffee shop on weekdays. "We'll see you inside."

Amber had already left the car. She homed in on the entrance that combined natural elements with sophisticated design. An obviously classy and expensive home, Amber was drawn like a magnet. When Uncle Walter opened the door, she set down the leather messenger bag she'd been carrying since she entered Reflections. She gracefully shook his hand and dipped, almost as though giving him a curtsy. "Love, love, love your work," she gushed.

"Thank you."

"I mean, I saw a display at the VanDusen in Manhattan that was fabulous."

The handsome elderly gentleman braced himself on a hand-carved ebony cane and smoothed the groomed line of his white beard. His gray fleece vest and jeans were spattered with clay, which meant he must have been working on the wheel in his back room rather than trekking to the studio in the snow. Keeping busy had always been Uncle Walter's way of dealing with problems. No matter how cool he pretended to be, Mallory knew he was worried about Gloria. He looked away from Amber and turned to Mallory. "Who is this?"

"Amber DeSilva. I'm Gloria's eldest daughter." She swept past him into the front foyer where four niches held small sculptures of the elements—earth, water, air and fire. Hundreds of reproductions of these artworks had been one of Walter Pulaski's greatest successes. Amber shivered and gasped and moaned as though having an art orgasm. "These must be the originals. Fabulous. These are worth a fortune. Can I touch them? Can I hold them?"

"They're not for you," Walter said quietly.

Mallory was more irritated by Uncle Walter's lack of surprise at Amber's introduction. He must be aware of the secrets in Mom's past. Why had he never told her? Everyone seemed to know more about her mother than she did. Shane had his internet research to keep him updated. Uncle Walter had memories of a different time. And Amber? Well, her sources of information were enigmatic.

Mallory needed to get to the bottom of this. As soon as Walter herded them into his dining room where his housekeeper had placed a coffee service with lox, cream cheese and bagels on a side table, she squared off with Amber.

"Before we go any further," Mallory said, "I think you owe me some evidence. You've made a lot of claims but have given me no reason to trust you."

"You want proof?"

"That's right." Mallory stood toe to toe with her sister,

wishing she was six inches taller so she could look Amber straight in the eye. "I never saw you before this morning. How do I know you're telling the truth?"

Amber scoffed. "Do you mean to tell me…that the thugs who chased us through a blizzard and put a couple of bullets in your boyfriend's car…aren't proof enough?"

"Not my boyfriend." *Not that I'd mind if he was.* "Shane Reilly is a private eye. The chase and the gunfire happened after those people in the Hummer spotted your rental car at Reflections. Which only proves somebody is after you."

"Me?" Amber rolled her eyes and looked toward Walter Pulaski, the man she'd been fawning over. She didn't want to offend him. Even by Aspen standards, the internationally renowned sculptor was Richie Rich. Amber tried to look innocent. "Why would anybody chase me?"

"You're the one talking about stolen diamonds." Mallory backed off a step. "Look, I don't want to fight. But I need proof that Gloria stole the Teardrop, and now— twenty-six years later—she's trying to sell it."

Amber stalked to the end of the satin-smooth teak table with hand-carved legs. The heels of her boots clacked on the polished marble floor. She flipped open the flap on her leather messenger bag. "Mommy's art gallery didn't do well during the pandemic, did it? Reflections is running out of cash, and Gloria needs a great big infusion. Tell her, Pulaski."

Grasping a coffee mug in his calloused hand, he sank heavily into the seat at the head of the table. Mallory studied the scowl on his lined face. Why was he hesitating? What secrets did he know? Years ago, he'd taken over the accounting responsibilities for Reflections because Gloria sucked at math and was somewhat irresponsible. *Some-*

what? Change that to wildly irresponsible. In the circus of life, her mother soared like a spangled trapeze artist while Walter Pulaski was the strongman doing all the heavy lifting, leaving Mallory to play the role of a clown. "Uncle Walter?"

Nervous, he stroked his groomed white beard. "Is it warm in here?"

"Not really. There's nearly a foot of new snow outside."

And yet, he was sweating. He rolled up his shirtsleeves, spread his hands and gestured widely with the muscular forearms of a sculpture artist who chiseled beauty from chunks of granite. "The finances aren't so bad. Even if they were, I promise I'll always take care of you and Gloria. Always. And I'll never let Reflections close down."

Mallory caught the painful undercurrent of what he was saying. They were losing money and the gallery might go out of business. "We're broke."

She left the table, went to the wide triple-paned window and stared into the continuing snowfall. She should have paid more attention to the business end of the gallery. Her mom had never turned down a request for a new expenditure and had run up outrageous costs of her own by bringing in exhibitions from Chihuly, the glass blower, and a graffiti show featuring Banksy, who Gloria claimed to have dated. Maybe she really did have sex with the famously anonymous artist and many, many others. Mallory wasn't often shocked by anything her mom did, but she expected Walter to be straight with her.

As soon as she found her mom, Mallory intended to hire a real lawyer to replace the current guy who traded legal advice for the opportunity to show his paintings of oddly crossbred animals, like a turtle-ostrich or a camel-zebra.

Then she would gently ease Uncle Walter out of his job as an unqualified accountant. Everything would be okay when she found Gloria. If she found Gloria…

Tears tickled the backs of her eyelids. More than anything—the money, the art, the diamonds from Africa—Mallory missed her mother.

"Here's proof." Amber pointed to the screen of the laptop she'd taken from her bag. "This is a screen grab, shot three days ago from surveillance outside a pawnshop in Brooklyn. The owner of the shop, Ben Hooker, is a well-known fence, specializing in blood diamonds from Africa."

Staring at the screen, Mallory saw a red-haired woman on the sidewalk. She wore a long beige trench with a scarf in a vivid blue, orange and green pattern—a scarf just like it should be hanging in Gloria's closet. In the screengrab photo, the redhead had just taken off her sunglasses and was staring directly into the camera. There was no mistaking her identity.

"Three days ago," Mallory said.

"That's correct."

Mallory had found her mother.

Still missing but not dead.

Chapter Five

Shane tramped up the neatly shoveled sidewalk with Elvis bouncing beside him, trying to catch snowflakes on his long pink tongue. They paused at the sculpture of the giant woman in a turban rising from the earth and reaching for the sky. Though snow draped across her brow and the bridge of her nose, he saw Mallory in her ecstatic expression. Loving the sky. Open to nature. Had she been the model for this statue? Or had it been Gloria?

Elvis had the good taste not to pee on the artwork. Instead, he went to a clump of leafless aspens near the entrance.

From what Shane had learned online over the past few days, he saw beyond the similarities of mother and daughter and recognized their differences. Both possessed vitality, willingness to take risks and joy in living, but Mallory was more mindful. Though reaching for the stars, her feet remained firmly rooted. She'd organized the search for her mother with the skill of a general deploying troops for battle. Mallory set goals and fulfilled them. Unlike Gloria, she avoided being the center of attention and hid from the spotlight. During the time he'd spent with Mallory, Shane hadn't heard her talk about herself. Not once did she mention her own dreams and desires.

He wanted to open that Pandora's box, to know her on a deeper level, to understand what went on inside her head behind the breathtaking turquoise eyes. But he wasn't sure he could continue along this path, ignoring the glaring fact that Gloria had broken the law when she faked her death twenty-six years ago and stole a fortune in precious gems. Not unless he knew why she'd done it.

For sure, this was the most interesting investigation he'd had since getting his PI license, but he knew better than to sidestep the law, especially since they were being pursued by thugs in ski masks. He had to assume a firm stance, had to take control, to tell Mallory no. He couldn't work for her. Not unless she talked to the authorities. Though he liked to believe he could provide all the protection she needed, he wanted to be able to call for backup.

As he approached the carved entryway, the door whipped open. Mallory jumped out, threw her arms around his neck and planted a powerful kiss on his mouth. Too shocked to do anything but react, his arms coiled around her and lifted her feet off the floor. Not light as a hummingbird but solid and real, her slender body pressed tight against his chest. She was toasty warm and smelled like coffee. He allowed himself to accept and savor her wild burst of passion while it lasted, which wasn't long. She bounced away from him.

Beaming, she said, "She's alive. Gloria is alive."

When Mallory reacted on a purely emotional basis, she was ferocious and unstoppable. He couldn't say no to her. His resolution to immediately talk to the police melted like an ice sculpture in a sauna. He cleared his throat and said, "What brought you to this conclusion?"

"Amber has a photo, taken three days ago."

"And you're sure it's Gloria."

"As if I don't know my own mother."

He stepped into the foyer and closed the door. "I didn't mean to suggest—"

"Never mind." She dashed into a lavish dining room to the right of the entrance where she confronted Walter Pulaski, who stood at a side table filling his coffee mug. Mallory jabbed her finger at his chest. "You knew about Mom. Her history."

"I did," he admitted as he hobbled to the chair at the head of the long teak dining table. "I met her when she was in her teens. We hit it off, stayed in touch. Then she came to me when she was in her early twenties. Right before she changed her name."

"More proof." Amber pumped a fist in the air. "Walter is a witness to our mother's name change from Ingrid DeSilva."

Shane could think of several valid and sensible reasons for a name change. This bit of evidence represented the least devastating piece of the puzzle. He faced the white-haired man whom he'd met once before and liked. "Nice to see you again, Walter."

"Same to you, Shane. A devoted skier like yourself must be happy about the snow."

"The start of the season is always a cause for celebration." He'd think about skiing later. Right now, he concentrated on being a private eye. "What happened all those years ago when you saw Gloria?"

He nodded slowly, remembering. "She came to me here in Aspen and asked for help. I hardly knew her, but I couldn't refuse this fascinating creature. She was a goddess—a pregnant goddess. I might have been in love with her."

"I thought you were gay," Amber said.

"I'm an artist, fascinated by the female form. Gloria was my muse. And we had a good partnership. We both benefited. After she took over the sale of my sculptures, I began to profit royally. And she earned enough in commissions to open Reflections."

"You were royally successful," Shane said. "And Gloria had savings of her own."

"Quite a healthy nest egg."

Shane had heard this story before, but he recalled that Mallory mentioned current financial problems. "What happened to the money?"

"That was twenty-six years ago. Things change." Walter shrugged. "When the economy suffers, the purchase of art is one of the first things to go. I'm fortunate. My sales—especially the reproductions—are still doing well. But gallery owners, like Gloria and Mallory, take a risk with every new artist they spend money on to promote."

Elvis sidled through the door to the dining room. Before the dog could shake, rattle, roll and splatter snow all over the place, Shane dropped a towel he'd been carrying over the Lab's back and gave him a rub down. "Sorry, Walter, I should have done this the minute we came inside. He smells like wet dog."

"Perfectly natural."

Shane turned to Mallory. "In case you're wondering, my Navigator wasn't seriously damaged. Only four bullet holes in the left rear fender. The guys in the Hummer aren't great shots."

Walter Pulaski turned his chair, leaned forward with his elbows braced on his knees and smiled at Elvis. "I've been thinking about getting a dog."

"I recommend it," Shane said. "Forgive me for bringing this up, but the last time we visited I noticed you have a limp."

"Knee surgery."

"I'm no stranger to PT and rehab. That's where Elvis and I met. He was my therapy dog—the only one who believed I'd learn to walk and ski again."

"How does a dog help you to walk?"

"There's a whole range of AAT, Animal-Assisted Therapy. Much of the procedure is based on motivation. Working with a dog makes the boring repetition of therapy exercises less tedious. A larger dog like Elvis can be fitted with a special harness and trained to hold a position and provide a solid base for you to balance. They can help in all kinds of ways. Let me give you a quick demonstration."

Shane waved Elvis toward the chair where Walter was sitting and introduced them. With an expression that seemed both friendly and compassionate, Elvis held up his paw to shake hands.

"After you pet him for a while," Shane said, "have a conversation using his name. Be sure to tell Elvis that he's smart and good-looking. Flattery will get you everywhere."

Amber elbowed her way into their conversation. "Excuse me, but I have more evidence, important evidence."

"Not now." Shane held up his hand, signaling her to stop. Amber had inherited her mother's love of center stage, but he refused to be sucked into a conversation with her as the star, not until he was ready. "We're in the middle of something with Elvis."

"Really?" She huffed. "You'd rather pay attention to your dog?"

So true. Shane nodded to Walter. "I saw your cane

hanging near the front door. In a conversational way, tell Elvis to get it for you."

Uncle Walter looked into the dog's attentive face and said, "Elvis, I'd like to go for a little walk. Would you, please, be so kind as to fetch my cane for me?"

"Repeat the important words," Shane said.

"Please. Bring me the cane."

Elvis cocked his head to one side as though logging the information into his brain. Then he turned in a circle, raised his nose in the air and pranced toward the entry where Walter's cane hung on a coatrack. Delicately, Elvis lifted the cane in his teeth, carried it across the room and placed it on Walter's lap.

Mallory, Walter and Shane applauded while Elvis thumped his tail on the polished marble floor, tossed his head and gave his trademark sneer.

"Thanks, Elvis," Walter said. "You're a champ. I'm definitely going to look for a dog like you. Any suggestions for where I should start?"

"I'll hook you up," Shane said. "Not that I'd try to influence you, but Elvis is partial to lady poodles—long-legged standard poodles with curly hair."

Amber groaned. "Are we done setting up a dating service for your dog? Do you think we can get back to the multi-million-dollar business at hand?"

"Fine." Mallory pulled out a chair, set her coffee mug on the table and sat. "It seems that you've had zero contact with Gloria over the years. How did you know she'd gone missing? Why did you come looking for her and for me?"

Amber sat opposite. She reached out with a manicured fingernail and pointed at the laptop screen photograph of Gloria with red hair. "I received this picture with a message to contact Ben Hooker, the pawnshop owner I mentioned earlier. Though I hadn't seen her in person since I was a child, I recognized our mother. She still looks very much like the old photos from Sierra Leone that Felix showed me. I barely knew her. Thought she was dead. The pictures were all I had."

Though he didn't like Amber, Shane was touched by the story of an abandoned child who had lost her mother. When he saw the tears brimming in Mallory's eyes, he knew she felt the same. "Amber, have you stayed in touch with Felix?"

"Of course. He's more like family than my blood relatives. He lived with us almost full-time until I was eighteen and went off to college. As I got older, I realized that he paid for many things that my dad or grandma said were too expensive for a young girl. As if they had any idea what was suitable for me. Felix knew. He gets me. He understands."

"Is he wealthy?" Shane asked.

"He inherited," Amber said. "And he earns a decent amount of money from his original artwork, especially the carved painted masks based on traditional tribal designs."

Mallory's spine stiffened. "Felix Komenda. I know him. We handle his sales at Reflections."

"It's the least our mother could do for him. From what I understand, she never would have gotten away from Sierra Leone without his help."

"So Felix knew all along that Gloria wasn't dead. And he never told you. Or me."

"He was loyal to Gloria."

Walter spoke up. "Your mother was in danger. If certain people found out she was still alive, they would have come after her."

"Like this Conrad person," Shane said. This complicated, intriguing story had taken them very far afield, and he reminded himself that the entire yarn hung on the childhood memories of Amber, who couldn't be trusted as a reliable source. "What happened after you contacted the fence?"

"Ben Hooker promised top dollar if I delivered the African Teardrop to him. After Ingrid or Gloria or whatever she's calling herself visited him, she pulled another vanishing act."

"Did she ever show him the Teardrop?"

"No."

"Did she tell him where it was?"

"No."

This series of events had taken an illogical turn. If Gloria had the diamond, it made sense for her to hand it over to Hooker when she first met with him or make arrangements to deliver the Teardrop shortly thereafter. Was it possible that she'd lost the precious stone? "Did Hooker demand proof? Why look for a buyer if he wasn't one hundred percent sure she had the stone?"

"She showed him photos on her phone with the diamond resting on a newspaper. You know, like kidnappers do with ransom victims."

He wondered if the pictures were taken in New York. "Which newspaper?"

"*USA TODAY.* The date was proof. The location could be anywhere."

Mallory pursued their interrogation from a totally different direction. "You've got me worried again. We know

Mom was okay in that photo with the red wig, before she disappeared again. How do we know she's still all right?"

"She calls Hooker. And she sent a photo of herself in Denver to prove she's still alive."

Mallory perked up. "So she's in Colorado."

"I suppose." Amber scowled. "She's doing this wild dance to keep Hooker on the line, but he's not amused. He'd rather deal with me than her or any of the other dangerous people after the diamond."

"So you made friends with Hooker," Mallory said, summarizing. "How did that lead to me?"

"Like I told you before, once I had the name Gloria Greenfield, I tracked you down. Your website is absolutely full of inquiries about your missing mother, which backed up Hooker's story. And there were also pictures of you. Well, I took one look and—" Amber framed her own face with her fingers "—I knew. You were the fetus our mother was carrying when she disappeared from Sierra Leone."

Shane still had questions. Why would Gloria keep checking in with a pawnbroker in Brooklyn? Had she come to Denver? Where was the diamond? He looked to Walter for explanations. "Does this sound plausible to you?"

He gave a slow sad nod. "It's not reasonable but utterly possible. Gloria has never been known for making well-considered plans. She's impulsive."

"If she has the diamond, why doesn't she move forward to sell it?"

"She might have lost it." Walter spread his hands, palm up, as if making an offering to the gods. "It seems inconceivable, but I can think of dozens of other scenarios. Maybe she gave it to a friend to hold. Or buried it and forgot where she dug the hole. She might have decided not to sell it, after all, and return it to its rightful home. At one time, the Teardrop was considered a national treasure belonging to Sierra Leone."

"What?" Amber shrieked. "Give it back? Never!"

"That's what we should do," Mallory said. "Return the stone to the rightful owner."

"Don't be absurd."

"First we need to find it." Shane struggled to bring order to the chaos that seemed to infect Gloria's plans. "We'll start with the safe-deposit box. Mallory, show Walter the key."

She reached into her jeans pocket and pulled out the key they'd found at Gloria's house. "Uncle Walter, do you know which bank this belongs to?"

Frowning, he studied the key. "She uses Fidelity United Bank here in town. She chose it for the initials."

"FU," Shane said.

"Exactly," Walter responded. "And there's another bank in Denver. Can't recall the name but I can look it up."

"We'll start here with FU." Shane was glad to have some kind of direction. "Then we'll go to Reflections and make a more thorough search."

Amber stood and looked down her nose at them. "Aren't you forgetting something? We have a gang of armed thugs in ski masks chasing after us."

"I sure as hell haven't forgotten." Shane's wary brain sent out constant warning signals, keeping him on edge. "I'm still in favor of calling the police for protection."

"Can't do it," Mallory said. "Mom would end up in jail."

"Absolutely can't," Amber chimed in. "Not that I particularly care about Gloria being arrested. But I'm sure the police would confiscate the Teardrop, and we'd be out millions of dollars."

"One of you stands for love. The other for greed," Shane said. "Two powerful emotions. Neither of you will give in."

"Not a chance," the two women said with one voice.

"I have one nonnegotiable condition." Disregarding Amber, he concentrated on Mallory. "Until this is resolved and Gloria is found, I will act as your bodyguard. All day and all night."

An enticing little grin curved her mouth. "I accept your terms, Shane. It's you and me, together. Twenty-four hours a day."

Bring it on.

Chapter Six

Wondering if Shane was worried about what he'd just gotten himself into, Mallory held his gaze. His dark eyebrows and thick lashes emphasized the honey-brown color of his eyes. His cheeks were still ruddy from being out in the snow. He radiated confidence. No matter what life threw at him, Shane came out a winner.

She enjoyed looking at him, and the prospect of having him with her day and night was super appealing, especially at night when they'd have to stay close together. Sharing the same meals, the same bed or the same shower. Her breath caught in her throat. She had to change her focus before she slid all the way down the rabbit hole into an impossible wonderland. Too many other issues to consider. His undeniable charm didn't count for much when dealing with her mother's disappearance and the loss of the African Teardrop. More than anything, he had to be a good enough detective to solve this puzzle.

The phone in her pocket chimed. When she saw the name *Sylvia* on caller ID, Mallory cringed. Should have called Sylvia earlier. Her good friend and coworker for the past six years tended to be easily excitable, a trait that her new husband found adorable. Mallory wasn't so delighted with semi-hysterics. With a resigned sigh, she answered the phone. "I'm sorry that I didn't—"

"There's blood on the kitchen floor," Sylvia shouted in a high nervous voice, nearly a banshee shriek. "Blood. Both doors are unlocked, front and back. A tray of coffee mugs is scattered on the floor, displays in the front are messed up."

Though Sylvia might be overreacting, a bolt of fear shot through Mallory. What if the bad guys were still there? It hadn't occurred to her that they might stick around or come back to Reflections, but that was a definite possibility. "Listen to me, Sylvia. It's best if you get out of there. Right away."

"Did I mention the blood!"

"Lock up and go home."

"I'm calling Brock."

The police chief. "No, please don't do that."

"Something terrible has happened."

"You're right about that, and it's connected to Mom's disappearance." Mallory heard a string of unintelligible curses from her friend who wasn't one of Gloria's greatest fans. "Getting the authorities involved will only make things worse. Trust me on this. Please."

"I'm not going to turn tail and run, and I won't drag the police into this. But I'm calling Damien. He can be here in ten minutes, and he'll protect me."

Damien Harrison, her husband of four months, stood as tall as Shane and was forty pounds heavier. His extra weight was solid muscle. He managed a horse ranch and was a professional cowboy. He'd won the bronco busting competition two years running at Frontier Days in Cheyenne. For sure, Damien could keep his wife safe.

"We'll be there as soon as we can," Mallory promised.

"We? Who's with you?"

"Shane Reilly, the private investigator." How could she explain Amber? "And someone you've never met before. See you soon. Be careful."

She disconnected the call before Sylvia could ask more probing questions. Explaining Amber was going to be a problem. Uncle Walter had accepted her without hesitation, which might be because he was more familiar with Gloria's checkered past. Sylvia would be judgmental, as would most of Mallory's friends and associates who considered Gloria to be an irresponsible twit. They didn't see her as a single mother who had struggled to establish a business in a highly competitive field while raising a daughter. Mallory couldn't waste time worrying about other people's opinions.

She turned toward Shane and Amber. "We need to get back to Reflections. Sylvia showed up for work, and she's there alone."

"I heard you tell her to leave," Shane said.

"And she refused. Her husband, Damien, is coming to protect her and ought to be there in just a couple of minutes."

"Damien Harrison," Shane said. "He's a big guy and tough as they come, but the men who attacked us were armed."

If something happened to Sylvia or any of her other employees, Mallory would be devastated. "What should I do?"

"Close Reflections until this is over."

Though it went against her instincts as a business owner to shut down, especially after their forced time off during the pandemic, she knew he was right. She immediately called Sylvia back and told her to go home because she was shutting down Reflections for the immediate future. She'd send out an email blast to everybody who worked there, making an excuse for the lockdown. Something about repairs or plumbing. She ended with, "Please don't tell anybody about the blood."

"Not even Damien?"

"Only if he promises not to tell anybody else."

"As if he's some kind of gossip?" Sylvia laughed at the idea of her macho husband chitchatting with the other cowboys at the ranch.

"You're right. My secret is safe with him."

"Before I go, I'll post a closed sign at the door and turn out the lights."

"Thanks, I'll stay in touch."

When she ended her call, she saw that Shane already had his phone in hand. "Just in case, I'm calling Damien. He'll make sure his wife is tucked away safely."

"How do you know Damien Harrison?"

"We've got a lot in common. Until Damien started dating your friend, we were both single guys in Aspen."

Mallory caught the gist of his comment. Many of the hot local guys ran in the same circles, drank in the same taverns and dated the same women. She shuddered. Not a pleasant thought.

He continued, "We're both athletes. Different venues, but we'd run into each other doing weight training."

"Of course." A skier and a rodeo cowboy had more similarities than differences. Maybe they were working on different sets of muscles, but they both needed to stay in shape. Aspen was that kind of town: obnoxiously healthy.

Mallory followed her own physical regimen—jogging, weights, yoga and tai chi—even though she wasn't a competitive sportswoman.

Turning away from him, she concentrated on shutting down Reflections for what she hoped would be a limited time. She changed the message on the phone and with the answering service to say they'd be closed for a while and wouldn't be able to return calls for a few days. Next, she contacted her employees. Using her phone she sent out a text and an email saying that Reflections would be closed for a few days, maybe a week, due to repair work. She added that they'd be paid for their time off and ended with, Enjoy the snow.

Collapsing in her chair at Uncle Walter's dining table, she checked the time. It was only 9:52 a.m., but she felt like she'd already put in a full day's work. She glanced toward Amber, who perched on a chair near Uncle Walter and lavished him with praise while he sat sipping his coffee and sketching in a five-by-eight notebook. Mallory really didn't want to drag Amber along with them while they searched at Reflections and went to the bank to check the safe-deposit box. Her complaining and superior attitude were a drag, to say the least.

She looked over at Shane. "Earlier this morning, you said you'd dug up more information on Mom."

"Knowing about her change of identity pretty much explains my online investigating. I found no records for Gloria Greenfield before you were born. A shallow attempt was made to create an alternate background with a high school and art school, but it didn't take much research to figure out that her alleged history was bogus. I'll go back and search for info on Ingrid DeSilva. That might give us a clue for where she's hiding."

"What kind of clue?"

"She could be staying with friends or family she knew before she became Gloria." He went to the side table and poured himself another cup of coffee. "I'll check it out."

"Really? Do you think I have more family that I'm not aware of?"

"Maybe."

The idea shocked her. Finding out about her missing sister had been a major surprise, but a whole family? Mallory had grown up with no reference to grandparents, aunts, uncles or cousins. According to Gloria, the two of them were alone in the world. "Why wouldn't Mom tell me about them?"

"My guess? She thought she was protecting you. The less you knew about her criminal past, the better."

So many emotions churned inside her. Mallory couldn't sit still. She rose from the dining table and returned to the wide bay window that looked out at the giant statue of Gloria reaching for the sky through the continuing snowfall. Elvis sat beside her, and she stroked his still-damp fur. Had Mom lied to her about everything? Mallory paced toward the corner where a white marble statue on a pedestal—Gloria breastfeeding—greeted her. In Uncle Walter's house, Mom was inescapable. She dominated his art and his memories. Had friends and family from her earlier life felt the same way? Would they welcome her home with open arms?

Mallory struggled to regain her balance and pull herself together. When she heard Amber giggle, she turned her head and saw her alleged sister preening for Uncle Walter. Obviously, she wanted him to use his renown and talent to sculpt her. *Too obviously.* If Amber had asked for her advice, Mallory could have told her that nobody coerced Uncle Walter into taking on a project that didn't interest him. Not even commissioned jobs. His last major project was a life-size memorial for his good buddy, Hunter S. Thompson, with a cigarette dangling from the corner of his mouth and a Colt .45 revolver held close to his vest. Mallory loved the statue. The whirling grain of the stone suggested the hazy thinking of the gonzo journalist. The lenses on his glasses were mirrors that reflected the viewer in a disturbing way.

Amber giggled again. "What are you drawing, Walter? Is it me?"

He frowned, ran his fingers through his beard and gave a noncommittal grunt.

"It is." She clapped her hands. "You're making a sketch of me."

"Not you." He turned his drawing pad around so she could see the picture he'd been working on. "It's the dog."

He'd captured the bright intelligence of the Lab and the Elvis-like smirk on his upper left lip. "I love it," Mallory said.

"I have a chunk of black marble I've been itching to use."

His focus on the sketch told her that his attention had shifted to his art, which didn't work well for her. She needed his thoughts and memories tied to Mom. "You knew Gloria when she was Ingrid DeSilva. Did she mention family or friends?"

"Don't think so. And she wasn't married to DeSilva when we first met. Her name was Ingrid Stromberg or something like that. No family. There was a young man

with her, but he faded quickly from sight. I don't even recall his name. Why are you asking about long ago?"

"She could be contacting people from her past. People
she might have kept in touch with over the years. She did
a lot of traveling. Business trips, you know. And she went
to New York twice a year."

"Where I live," Amber said without her usual bluster.
Knowing that Walter preferred the dog over her had deflated
her ego. "I can promise you that she wasn't visiting me."

"What about our, um, father?" Mallory steeled herself
for what might come next. She'd spent her entire life believing her father was dead. "Would she turn to him?"

"Not unless she had a death wish," Amber said. "He
hated her. Cursed her memory."

Mallory couldn't blame her for the harsh tone. She'd
grown up motherless, abandoned by Gloria. "I'm sorry
for what you went through."

"Save your pity for someone who needs it. My life
wasn't bad at all. I lived with my grandpa and grandma
DeSilva in a tall narrow Manhattan townhouse that had
been in the family for generations. Like your mother, Dad
traveled a lot, but Felix was always there for me. He lived
on the fourth floor and had a studio where he did his
painting."

Mallory made a mental note to track down Felix Komenda. "What else can you tell me about our father? How
old is he? What does he look like?"

"There's not much more to tell." Genuine emotion
tugged at the corners of her mouth. For a moment, she
showed her grief. "He died in Africa a few years ago.
Murdered."

Her voice softened to a husky whisper as though telling

this story to herself. But the others were paying rapt attention. Shane, Walter and even Elvis watched her as she continued, "The thug who killed Dad worked for Conrad Burdock."

"The man who's after Gloria," Shane said.

"My, my, you catch on quick." Her hostile attitude was back in full force. "Burdock is a terrible human being, a mercenary who fled to Africa to avoid prosecution in the United States, and I'm certain he was behind Dad's murder. The guy who actually committed the crime claimed he was hired by Burdock."

"Do the police have the murderer in custody?" Shane asked.

"He's dead." She flashed a hard satisfied smile. "The worm got what he deserved."

Mallory had the wretched feeling that Amber had arranged for the death of the assassin hired by Burdock. Maybe she'd even pulled the trigger.

Amber spun the laptop around and tapped on the keys. The screen showed a snapshot of a handsome man wearing a custom tuxedo. His dark hair was combed straight back from his high forehead and streaked with gray at the temples. His eyebrows and mustache were black. His hazel eyes stared with a ferocious intensity that some women would find sexy. Not Mallory. To her, he looked mean.

Amber gestured gracefully as she introduced him. "This is Raymond DeSilva."

Their father. Mallory saw nothing of herself in his features. His mouth sneered. His angry eyes accused her of doing something wrong before she'd even said hello. Still, she wished she'd had the opportunity to meet him, to hear his voice and discover why her Mom had found him attractive.

Amber took the laptop back and punched in a new code. Another photo came up. "This is Conrad Burdock."

This time, Mallory recognized the face on the screen. A few days ago, just before she hired Shane, Conrad Burdock came to Reflections and spoke to her about purchasing one of Uncle Walter's sculptures of Gloria.

Chapter Seven

Their search had swerved into a disturbing new direction, and Shane didn't like the look of the road around that corner. Danger pointed directly at Mallory. Her encounter with Burdock—a man he was beginning to think of as some kind of evil mastermind/supervillain—represented a clear threat. He wanted to bring in the Aspen police, the Pitkin county sheriff and maybe the National Guard—whatever it took to protect her. But she refused. Her logic: Burdock hadn't harmed her when he'd had the chance, which meant she wasn't really in danger. Shane thought otherwise.

With Mallory in the passenger seat and Elvis in the back, he drove his Navigator through the sputtering end of the storm. Fat white flakes fell in batches and swirled through the air rather than joining together in a nearly impenetrable curtain. They were headed toward Reflections to search for the Teardrop among the art displays.

He cleared his throat. "I'm going to call my brother in Denver."

"The cop?" Her eyes widened in alarm.

"Don't worry. I won't tell him about the stolen diamonds or any of your mom's other crimes. I need his help with research."

"What kind of research?"

"The local police and I worked together to track the usage of Gloria Greenfield's credit cards. Not a difficult task because we had access to all her records, identification numbers and passwords. As you know, we found nothing. The day your mom disappeared, she stopped charging her expenses and left no record of buying plane, train or bus tickets."

"You think she might be using an alternate identity, like Ingrid DeSilva," Mallory said. "If not DeSilva, Uncle Walter said her maiden name might be Stromberg."

"If we get a nibble on those aliases, we'd have a clue as to her whereabouts. Unfortunately, I don't have the legal authority to quickly put my hands on confidential records."

"But your brother does."

"Logan has helped me before." And wasn't happy about skirting the edges of the law for his private eye brother. Still, both Logan and their father would do just about anything to encourage Shane's pursuit of a more stable profession than "former professional skier who might be talked into extreme life-threatening adventures." The fact that they considered private investigating to be a relatively safe occupation said a lot about his family's values.

He drove his 4WD Navigator past Reflections where the only vehicle in the parking lot was Amber's snow-covered rental SUV. Fading tire tracks showed where Sylvia had come and gone. There was no sign of the men in ski masks.

After circling a few blocks, he maneuvered the Navigator through the accumulated snow outside Mallory's house where he managed to park in the driveway. In addition to searching, they had a number of other projects, and he was glad they'd talked Amber into staying at Uncle Walter's house. Hadn't taken much convincing; she was delighted to lounge in the lap of luxury while they schlepped through the storm.

"Bring a small suitcase," he said. "Pack enough for a couple of days at my place."

"I still don't understand why we can't stay here."

"Do you have an alarm system on your house?"

"No."

"How about weapons and ammo?"

"I used to have a hunting rifle. But now? *Nada*."

"What kind of search engine do you have on your computer?"

She threw up her hands. "Okay, I get it. Your place is better prepared for detective work and more well-protected."

"Also there's space for Elvis to roam, plus all his food and other supplies."

"Fine," she agreed with a resigned sigh. "We'll stay at your cabin."

He didn't usually have this much trouble convincing women to come home with him, and he very much wanted to have her willing consent. Though she sounded annoyed about spending the night with him, he wondered, *Was she, really?* A couple of times, he'd caught her watching him from the corner of her beautiful turquoise eyes. She often smiled and laughed at his silly jokes. And then, there was that kiss. She'd planted one on him, supposedly because she was happy to discover her mom was alive, but he sensed a deeper connection between them.

"You'll like my house." He made direct eye contact. "And I'll like having you there."

An impatient whine from the back seat reminded him that Elvis wanted out. Pulling his watch cap over his hair, Shane stepped out of the Navigator and opened the door for his dog. Much as he loved the snow, he wasn't a fan of the cold that came with it. Not one of those guys who scampers around in a blizzard wearing board shorts and a tee, his winter clothing—from head to toe—was insulated and flexible, designed to keep him toasty and warm. He followed Mallory up the sidewalk.

Standing under the small gable roof over her front porch, she picked up a snow shovel and handed it to him. "While you're waiting for me, make yourself useful."

He grabbed the handle and muttered, "Shoveling the sidewalk isn't usually covered by my detective fee."

"Don't forget the driveway. Otherwise I'll have trouble getting out of the garage." She pivoted, unlocked the door and darted inside. "Should I bring anything from the kitchen?"

"I have food." His cabin was secluded but only a couple of miles away from an excellent organic grocery, and they delivered. "Just pack clothes and your lady bathroom products. I don't keep lotions and potions in stock."

"No scented candles for the bathtub?"

"I'm a shower guy. My tub is for hydrotherapy." Though the last remnants of the storm tumbled around them, his imagination filled with steam from the bath and Mallory rising naked from the water. Under his layers of clothing and parka, he began to sweat. "Twelve massage jets and a whirlpool. I'd be happy to show you how it works."

"And I'd be happy to let you."

Before she closed the door, she flashed a sexy smile and winked. Definitely, she was flirting. He couldn't be misreading these signals. Mallory liked him.

That conclusion kept him energized while he cleared the snow from the short sidewalk leading to the porch, the sidewalk in front and some of the driveway. Elvis bounded across her yard, burying himself in the snow and then standing and shaking it off. In a sudden change of pace, the dog stiffened the way he did when he'd made a find while doing search and rescue.

"What is it, boy?"

The dog sneered, growled and stared across the street.

Dropping the shovel, Shane looked in the direction Elvis indicated. He didn't see what had caused the reaction but feared there might be a threat. "Elvis, heel."

The Lab moved into position, standing at Shane's left hip and still staring. If the guys in the ski masks were back, Shane was in big trouble. The bad guys had gotten the drop on him, which was why bodyguards didn't do things like shovel walkways.

He should have concentrated on the task at hand, which was to protect Mallory. Should have gone into the house with her. Why was she taking so long? He tore off his glove to unzip his parka and reach for his gun.

Though Elvis stayed in the "heel" position, he wiggled and wagged his tail—too friendly for danger. He wasn't cool and determined like his namesake when he sang the lyric, "Are you looking for trouble?" Elvis the dog yipped. Across the street, a malamute appeared, took a stance and barked a greeting of his own.

"Are you kidding me?" Shane muttered. "Dude, we're not here to make friends."

Elvis gave him a skeptical look.

"You're right, I'm lying. I want to be friends with Mallory. More than friends." He stuck his gun into the holster, picked up the shovel and tramped back to the porch.

"Maybe then I'll stop trying to have meaningful conversations with a Labrador retriever. No offense."

Walking close beside him, the dog bobbed his head.

Shane entered without knocking. He'd visited Mallory's house before and liked her eclectic mix of classic and modern, similar to her mom's decor but not so chaotic. Some of the oil paintings were compelling, rich and beautiful. Others had been done by kids with finger paints and watercolors. In a seemingly unplanned manner, all the pieces fit together and created a charming whole. She was a master at setting up interesting little displays in ignored corners, using ceramics, origami, dried branches and yarn sculptures. Her home felt lived in. "Hey," he called out.

"In the dining room," she responded.

As he and Elvis went through the front room into the attached dining area, he asked, "Did you search for clues in your house?"

"First thing I did." Mallory sat at the head of the table and plucked at the keys on her laptop. "Mom bought this house when I was a baby, and she had plenty of time to hide grown-up stuff so I couldn't get my sticky little fingers on it."

"Find anything interesting?"

"Mostly keepsakes, like a shell from a beach in San Francisco and crystals from a cave on the Continental Divide. And jewelry, lots of costume jewelry."

"The African Teardrop? You were only a kid. Wouldn't know the difference between cubic zirconia and the genuine stone."

"That's not the way I was raised," she said. "Mom knew a lot about precious gems, and she taught me how to tell a real diamond from a fake."

"How?"

"You can tell by looking at it. Diamonds have more sparkle in a brighter spectrum. They don't get scratched but usually have flaws deep inside. You can see through a fake as though it was glass. And there's the water test."

"Tell."

"Fill a glass halfway with water. Drop the naked stone into it. If it sinks, it's a diamond. If it floats, it's fake."

And she'd learned all this when she was a kid. "You had an interesting childhood."

"There are advantages to having a weirdo mom."

On the floor beside her chair was an extra-large, expandable backpack. The thing looked big enough to carry the uniforms for the Colorado Avalanche hockey team, including their skates. "You're packed," he said.

"I should have come outside and joined you, but I had a few emails I needed to send."

He didn't believe that excuse. "More likely you wanted to stay inside while I finished shoveling. Otherwise, you could have taken the laptop with us, and we'd be on our way."

"Or I'm such a good employer that I feel an immediate obligation to the people who work for me and the suppliers who come every day—rain, shine or blizzard—with supplies for the coffee shop. Maybe I'm such a good teacher that I needed to notify the kids in my afternoon classes that we wouldn't be meeting for the rest of the week."

Elvis rubbed his red leather harness against the backpack, which was easily large enough for him to fit inside. Usually Shane was careful not to allow Elvis to drip all over somebody else's house, but he was irritated at her. "You teach?"

"Four classes with different age groups. We have a showing scheduled for next week at Reflections. All the parents come, and the kids show off for their friends from school. We have cheese and crackers and juice while we talk about colors and shadows."

He pointed to a framed picture on the wall that appeared to be a man on horseback who had lassoed a rocket ship. Everything was painted in shades of blue and purple. "Tell me how you'd analyze this technique."

"An outsize talent. Great metaphor." She grinned. "It's an astronaut cowboy reaching for a blue moon."

While she talked, the tension at the corner of her eyes relaxed, and the tone of her voice mellowed. He could tell she honestly enjoyed working with these kids. "Can anybody come to this showing? Or do I need a special invite?"

"I'd love to have you there. Elvis, too. He's well-behaved, and I know he'd be a hit with the kids." She stood and slipped into her parka. "I guess we ought to get going."

His natural instinct was to pick up her giant backpack and carry it for her, but he needed to be a bodyguard instead of a boyfriend. If weighed down by her luggage, he couldn't reach his gun quickly. And so he straightened his shoulders and walked unencumbered to her front door.

"I'm going onto the porch first," he informed her. "As your bodyguard, I want to check out the neighborhood and make sure it's safe before you come out."

She hefted her pack and nodded. "Whatever you say."

"When we leave here, I think we should go to the bank first."

"I'm with you. Even a total flake like Mom would have the good sense to keep something as precious as the Teardrop in a safe-deposit box instead of a hidey-hole at Reflections."

He didn't point out that the key to the box had been discovered in a secret cache at Gloria's house. "Let's hope so."

"We can only hope that this is the right bank."

On the porch, he stuck his Ray-Bans onto the bridge of his nose and scanned the street from left to right and back again. Two houses up the hill, a teenager shoveled the sidewalk. A Wagoneer chugged down the neighbor's driveway to the street. He saw no sign of the men in black ski masks or their massive Hummer, but he wouldn't let down his guard. It was too much to hope that supervillain Burdock had given up the hunt.

FIDELITY UNITED BANK occupied the first floor of a red-brick building with windows across the front, parking in back and a drive-through. Mallory had been here hundreds of times before. They used FU for deposits from Reflections, and she'd established a savings account for college when she was ten and Uncle Walter had given her a check for two hundred bucks. Several of the tellers and the bank manager knew her by name. Born and raised in Aspen, Mallory's roots went deep. She'd gone to high school here and was prom queen in her senior year. Practically all the locals had participated in the search for Gloria, and Mallory didn't anticipate any trouble accessing the safe-deposit box.

The snowfall had lessened, and people were getting started with their day while the plows cleared the main thoroughfares. According to weather reports, the upper slopes had gotten over eighteen inches of new snow. In town, they were looking at eight to ten inches overnight, which wasn't considered too hazardous. In the high Rockies, a minor blizzard didn't amount to a major threat.

On the other hand, her life was a nightmare and getting scarier by the minute. In the past few hours, she'd learned that her mother faked her own death, stole a precious diamond and was on the run. Mallory had confronted a sister who resented and hated her. As if that weren't enough, she'd been shot at, chased and stalked. At the moment, she could only think of one positive aspect, and that was Shane.

During the drive from her house, he acted like a professional bodyguard, diligently checking his rearview and side mirrors to make sure they weren't being followed. She also kept watch. He drove into the mostly empty parking lot, which had already been plowed, and parked near the entrance. "Before we go inside, Elvis needs a wardrobe change."

"Why?"

"Well, he's wearing his badass studded leather and looks like a tough guy. To go into the bank, he needs his service dog harness."

"Are you and Elvis coming with me to open the safe-deposit box?"

"I'm going to stay in the lobby so I can cut off any threat before it gets close to you. Also, I'm armed and don't intend to hand over my weapon."

He went around to the far back of the Navigator and rummaged until he found a red harness and matching leash, which he handed to her so she could help Elvis get changed. Shane posted himself at the back bumper and kept watch. Though she suspected this extreme level of vigilance might be over the top, Mallory appreciated her bodyguard. Never before had anyone devoted themselves to watching over her. With his dark sunglasses and alert posture, Shane looked like one of those secret service agents who protected VIPs and diplomats. She was neither but liked the attention.

While she unfastened Elvis's leather harness and put on the other, she was impressed with how the supposedly tough, fierce dog behaved. He wagged his tail and licked her cheek. When he was outfitted in his service dog vest, she picked up his leash and slung the small knapsack she used as a purse over her shoulder. "We're ready."

Shane escorted her through the front door and waited by the bank guard's post with Elvis while she strolled past the teller stations and went to an office at the rear of the bank. She peeked inside the open door and waved to the heavyset man with thick brown hair and heavy eyebrows. "Hey, Mr. Sherman."

"Howdy-doody, Mallory." The bank vice president bounded to his feet and came around his carved mahogany desk to envelope her in a hug. "Knock-knock."

"Who's there?"

"Could be a skier. Snow telling unless you open the door." He immediately launched into another one. "When the skier's car broke down, how did he get around?"

"Don't know."

"By icicle."

"Good one." She rewarded him with a quiet chuckle. He had a dozen jokes for every occasion, each worse than the one before, but he meant well. Their acquaintance went back several years to the time when she'd dated his son, Josh—a wide receiver for the Aspen High School football team, appropriately named the Skiers.

The banker gave her a concerned smile. "Any news on your mother?"

"Nothing definite."

"She dropped by my office just about a week ago."

To look into her safe-deposit box? Mallory waited for him to continue, but he was silent. She added, "I hired Shane Reilly to investigate."

Mr. Sherman shook his head and frowned. "Poor guy, how's he holding up?"

The clear inference was that Shane's injury and subsequent loss of his career as an Olympic athlete should have left him broken and devastated. She resented the attitude but understood where it was coming from. Josh Sherman blew out his knee in college and ended what might have been a chance to play in the NFL.

Still, she defended Shane. "He might turn out to be a better detective than a skier. Did you know that both his dad and his brother are Denver cops?"

"Well, I hope he finds Gloria for you."

"And that's why I'm here." She dug into the front pocket of her knapsack, pulled out the flat silver key with six digits and held it toward him. "Is this for a safe-deposit box at the bank?"

"Looks like one of ours, and isn't that a co-inki-dink? Your Mom wanted to open the box, too."

This was it! Mallory felt certain she'd solved the mystery of the diamond worth twenty million dollars. Mr. Sherman took the key from her trembling hand and returned to the swivel chair behind his impressive desk. "Let's check the number."

While he searched the screen of his desk computer, she concentrated on keeping her breath steady and her pulse calm. This could be momentous. The air in the bank seemed to press in around her. When she swallowed, her throat felt tight.

"Okey dokey," Mr. Sherman said. "I verified this is Gloria's key. And you are an authorized person to open the safe-deposit box."

Her heart thumped hard against her rib cage. "Can we do it now?"

"Sure thing." He beamed at her. "I need to have you sign a couple of standard forms, and then we can go into the basement."

A terrible thought occurred to her. "If I find something of value in the box, can I take it home with me?"

"That's an excellent question." He rose from his chair and moved toward her. "Since Gloria designated you as an authorized person—a surrogate for herself, if you will— whatever is in that box belongs to you. I might have even given it to you without the key, being as you're a friend of the family."

After signing a few forms, Mallory followed Mr. Sherman down the stairs into a windowless basement where she'd never been before. In spite of the carpeted floor and cheery yellow walls, it felt cold amid the many file cabinets. The few employees working in this area wore thick sweaters, which wasn't all that unusual considering the weather. At the far end of the room, she saw a metal vault door that required two special keys and a digital code to open. The young woman at the desk nearest the door joined Mr. Sherman while he went through the required procedures and chatted about his son whose real estate business was doing very well. "But he still hasn't settled down, never saw fit to get married and give us grandchildren. I seem to recall that you're single, too."

"Yes, sir, I am."

"Josh's mother and I surely wish something had developed between the two of you. You'd make a handsome couple."

Borderline inappropriate, but she smiled anyway. Though she and Josh had dated for several months, she'd never felt the breath-taking connection to him that had overwhelmed her from the moment she laid eyes on Shane. Mr. Sherman pulled open the door to the safe-deposit vault. Together with the clerk from the nearby desk, he stepped inside.

Mallory caught a glimpse of a large room with floor-to-ceiling lockers of various sizes. "Wow," she said. "I didn't think there'd be so many."

"We have more than average for a bank our size. Aspen is a small but wealthy community. Now, I'll have to ask you to wait here while we retrieve the proper container."

"Can you tell me when Gloria got this box?"

"I could look up the exact date for you, but it was about ten years ago. I remember because you and Josh had just started dating."

When he returned to the vault door, he was carrying a metal container, almost two feet long, which he passed to the clerk who had accompanied him. He relocked the vault and escorted her to a small room with a long table and three chairs. Mr. Sherman centered the long box that looked to be about fourteen inches wide on the table and stepped back.

"I have to lock you in, Mallory, but don't worry. When you're ready to leave, push the button by the door and someone will let you out." He patted her shoulder. "It was good to see you. Don't be a stranger."

As soon as the door closed, she flipped open the lid. The box appeared to be stuffed with nine-by-twelve brown envelopes marked with dates from twenty years ago to the present. *No diamond.* She fished around the envelopes, feeling around at the edges for a relatively small piece of jewelry. *Nothing but paperwork.* Carefully, she lifted each envelope out and felt the inside contents. *Damn it, Mom, what's this all about?*

Mallory opened the most recent envelope and found a letter addressed to Gloria. Dated a week ago, the letter ended with *I will see you in Colorado, my friend.* Signed with a flourish by Felix Komenda.

Chapter Eight

Against his better judgment, Shane gave in to Mallory's wishes and agreed to return to Walter Pulaski's chalet so she could talk to Amber. Driving through downtown, he noted the efficient snow removal from the streets and the sidewalks outside shops and businesses. Everything seemed to be returning to normal after the semi-blizzard. Blue sky peeked through the clouds above the slopes. On a typical weekday in Aspen, it should have been easy to solve the complicated human drama playing out in Mallory Greenfield's life. *Not so.* They had a lot to figure out before they put things right.

From what she'd told him, the letters from Gloria's safe-deposit box had been written by Felix Komenda. Most of them provided a narrative of Amber DeSilva's childhood and early teens, including details a mother would want to know. Apparently, Felix had performed more than nanny duties, and his talents extended beyond his artwork. He was a biographer.

Mallory shuffled through the file box given to her by a bank official to carry the brown envelopes. "The latest letters, especially the one from a week ago, don't mention Amber at all. Felix talks about returning a precious treasure."

"The African Teardrop," Shane said. "Returning it?"

"Doesn't make sense. Seems more like she intended to sell it," she said. "He also mentions a trip to Colorado."

"Has he been to Reflections before? Maybe to discuss the sale of his artwork."

"I've met him once or twice." While she pondered, Mallory absentmindedly twirled the loose tip of her long golden braid. "He's about as tall as you are and very thin. Shaved head. Tattoo sleeves on both arms. Across his chest is a huge tattoo of the famous Cotton Tree in Freetown, the capital of Sierra Leone. His skin is a light mocha, and the orange and green colors of his tats really stand out."

"Impressive," he said. "With that detailed description, I could pick him out of a lineup."

"Yeah, I'm not an artist, but I've got a good visual sense."

"Does the letter say when he'll arrive?"

"It's vague. He also mentioned the Museum of Nature and Science in Denver. Specifically, he talks about the gem exhibit and a guy who works there. His name is Ty Rivera. You've got to admit that these letters are the best leads we've gotten so far."

"The fact that your mother was planning to meet Felix somewhere in Colorado is a whole lot more specific than her cryptic departure note."

"I'll be back?" Mallory chuckled.

Finding the cache of correspondence had brightened her mood. But Shane wasn't amused. Gloria was hiding something from her daughter. In Shane's experience, secrecy led to lies and lies meant trouble. He needed to figure out how to control the threat.

She pulled an envelope from the middle of the box,

opened the flap and reached inside. "Seems like I shouldn't look at these."

"Why not?"

"Most of the stuff from earlier years is about Amber. It's intimate and private. She ought to be the person going through them."

"We're not prying," he said. "The letters are evidence. Besides, Gloria wanted you to find them. She designated you as an authorized person to open the box."

"Apparently, I signed a form." Under her knitted blue cap, her smooth forehead wrinkled. "I don't remember. Since I'm a part owner of Reflections, Gloria used to routinely give me a bunch of business-related stuff to review and sign. Did I ever take a look at it? Not really."

"I used to be the same way about paperwork. Not anymore."

"What happened?"

"After my ski accident, I was in a coma for three days. My brother was there when I woke up. As soon as the nurse gave the okay, he hugged me and blubbered like a baby. The first coherent thing Logan said was, 'Dude, you never changed your will.'"

Her eyebrows raised. "I don't mean to criticize your brother, but that's a little bit mercenary."

"No, he was smart to check it out. In the will, I left everything to a former girlfriend. That's *former* with a capital *F*. To say we had a bad breakup would be like calling World War II a minor altercation. I always meant to update the will but never got around to it." Logan was right about a lot of things, and Shane still needed to call him for help in tracking credit cards for his private eye work.

"Anyway, don't worry about violating Gloria's privacy. She saved that stuff for a reason."

Mallory lifted a photograph from the envelope. "So adorable. It's little Amber blowing out candles on a birthday cake. Eight candles. Her eighth birthday. I can't wait to show her. She's going to love it."

"What makes you think so?"

"These letters and photos prove that Gloria didn't just turn her back and walk away. She had Felix keeping an eye on her daughter. Mom cared about Amber. When she reads these letters, she'll know. And she'll be happier."

His impression of her prodigal sister was way more cynical. Not once had he heard Amber speak fondly of their mother. She'd come looking for Gloria with a loaded gun, which didn't strike him as the attitude of a person who was longing to make a connection.

While Mallory pored over the letters, pointing out Amber's good qualities, he scanned the winding road leading to Pulaski's château, looking for the Hummer and considering what else they could accomplish today. A search at Reflections was on the agenda. Also, they needed to track down some of Gloria's clients, close friends and former lovers—people she might have told about her plan to disappear. He added doctor and lawyer to the list. The number one, most important contact had to be Amber's former nanny, Felix.

When they approached the entrance where the gatekeeper kept watch, Shane glanced over at Mallory, who chirped a friendly greeting to Henry. He beamed and waved back. Everybody who knew her loved her. Apart from hair color and matching turquoise eyes, she was very different from her sister. Amber was colder than a blizzard and hard as granite, while Mallory was warm, sweet and kind without being saccharine. The best part of his plan for the day would be taking her home with him tonight.

He parked his SUV in the shoveled driveway outside Walter Pulaski's house. The last time they were here, he'd caught a glimpse of the housekeeper who laid out the breakfast spread and coffee before vanishing. He guessed that Pulaski's other employees—like the person who cleared the snow—were also ubiquitous and silent. When Shane first came home after rehab, he'd required that kind of assistance. He'd had a part-time physical therapist and a live-in housekeeper who cooked and cleaned. Both had done their jobs well, but he couldn't wait to get rid of them and have the cabin to himself. Just him and Elvis against the world, that was the way he liked it.

Amber answered the front door as though she was mistress of the house, but she didn't look happy. "Walter locked himself in the small studio at the back of the house," she said.

Smart man. "And left you in charge?"

"No need to sound so surprised. I've been running households since I was a kid. I've just been chatting with the housekeeper about lunch."

"Great," Mallory piped up. "I'm starved."

Shane gestured with the file box from the bank. "May we come in?"

Amber stepped out of his way. "Walter told me that when you returned, he wanted to see Shane and the dog."

A perfect excuse for a getaway. He carried the box of letters to the dining room table, set it down and turned toward the sisters. "I know how to get to the small studio. I'll take Elvis and leave you two with this."

Amber scowled and flicked her fingers against the cardboard. "What's in there?"

"The contents of Mom's safe-deposit box. Something she considered precious." Mallory took off the lid and pulled out one of the brown envelopes. "I think you're going to be happy to see these letters. They're all about you."

"Why would that make me happy?"

"Well, it shows she cares about you."

"Ha! More likely she felt guilty, which is exactly what she deserves. What kind of person abandons her only child? Letters aren't enough."

"In her letters, she mentions seeing you from a distance on her trips to New York."

"And never saying hello."

Shane stepped into the hallway and made his escape with Elvis following close behind. He tapped on the door to the working studio behind the home office and the kitchen. "It's us, Shane and Elvis."

The door opened inward. Braced on his ebony cane, Walter peered around the edge. "Are you alone?"

"Amber isn't with us if that's what you're asking."

Breathing a sigh of relief, the old man stepped aside and let them enter. The rest of the house was pristine and polished. In here, splashes of dried paint decorated the concrete floor, and the walls held dozens of rough sketches. A potter's wheel stood in one corner and an easel in another. Shelves and tables held supplies and models for future work in the big studio beside the garage. The earthy smell of dried clay mingled with the scent of burnt wood from the potbellied stove. Sunlight filtered through the many windows.

On a heavy center table, he'd been experimenting with

small canine figures in modeling clay to use as a basis for his sculpture of Elvis. He hobbled to a sink, leaned his cane against it and washed his hands. "Haven't found the pose I want yet. Do you mind if I take photos?"

"Elvis loves being the center of attention, like Amber... but in a good way."

Pulaski settled himself on a special stool with a back he could lean against. "Hard to believe she's Mallory's sister. They resemble each other physically and both have a lot of Gloria in them, but being with Mallory always makes me happy. Amber's a bitch."

Shane couldn't have said it better himself. "At the bank, a vice president found paperwork showing Mallory as a designated person to open the safe-deposit box. No diamonds inside, but there were hundreds of letters written by Felix Komenda to Gloria and talking about Amber as a child."

"She saved those?" He rolled down his sleeves and buttoned the cuffs. "I knew she kept in touch with Felix and trusted him to take care of the kid. She also sent money and made several trips to New York to see for herself how Amber was doing. Nearly broke her heart to leave that little girl behind."

"Is that so?" Shane still didn't have the impression that Gloria was a caring mother.

"You don't know the whole story," Walter said. "Felix told me that Gloria had been physically and mentally abused by her husband. If she hadn't run when she had the chance, he suspected Raymond DeSilva would've killed her."

His explanation put a different slant on Gloria's motivations, but Shane wasn't sure he could take her friend Walter's word for her mothering skills. "According to the letters, Felix planned to be in Colorado, which probably means Gloria will join him. I'd like to check in with some of her associates and find out if she's contacted them."

"Got any names?"

Shane rattled off the two that Felix had mentioned specifically. "Her lawyer might know something. And her doctor."

"Dr. Freestone." He grinned and reached over to stroke Elvis's square forehead. "He's known Gloria since Mallory was born. Far as I know, she doesn't have any medical problems, but he's a person she trusts."

"And the lawyer?"

"Don't bother. He's barely competent, and we've been talking about replacing him."

From the dining room, he heard the angry voices of Mallory and her sister. So much for the idea that Amber would be pleased about the letters from Felix. Shane took his phone from his pocket and prepared to contact his brother in Denver. "If you'll excuse me, I need to make a call."

Walter rose from the stool and used his cane to walk to the door. "You stay here. I'm going to check with Constance about lunch and have her bring it in here."

"Thanks, I've been thinking about food. Do you mind if Elvis comes with you to the kitchen?"

"I'd be honored."

Shane called his brother's cell phone and caught him at his desk in DPD's Major Crimes Division where he'd recently been transferred. Logan sounded happy to hear from him. After a quick update on his two kids in grade school—Shane's niece and nephew—and his bright, beautiful CPA wife, he tossed out the usual query. "So, baby brother, any closer to finding a lady and settling down?"

"I've been busy." He kept his attraction to Mallory to himself, not wanting to get his brother's hopes up. Besides which, lusting after a client was highly unprofessional. "I could use your help on an investigation."

"Why am I not surprised? Tell me what you need."

Without explaining any of the details about Gloria's disappearance, he asked his brother to check into possible aliases on credit cards or travel documents. "On a related issue, I'm trying to locate a man named Felix Komenda, originally from Sierra Leone."

"Is this about diamonds?"

"What?" Surprised by his brother's conclusion, Shane cleared his throat and forced himself to remain calm. "Why would you think that?"

"Conflict diamonds, buddy. West African countries are known for using those gems to fund insurrections. Come on, you ought to know that. You're the one who traveled the world."

"But you've got more experience in crime solving."

"Neither one of us Colorado boys need to get involved in international intrigue."

"Felix doesn't have anything to do with that." *At least, I hope not.* "He's been living in the US for over twenty years. He's an artist."

Logan agreed to make the inquiries for him, and Shane ended the call just as Mallory and Amber stormed into the studio like a double-edged blonde tornado. Both were talking. Loudly.

"Where's Walter?" Amber demanded.

Mallory appealed to Shane, "Don't you think it means something that Gloria kept track of Amber for all these years? She loved her daughter."

He recalled Walter's statement about Gloria being heart-broken, but he wasn't about to step into the middle of this sister versus sister argument. "It's hard to know what's going on in another person's mind."

"That's for damn sure," Amber snapped. "Connect the dots on this bit of illogic. She decided to fake her death and steal diamonds. Because she loved me? No way."

"Look at these photos. She kept them all."

Amber picked up the picture of herself and the birthday candles. "I remember my eighth birthday. Felix gave me a two-wheeler. All the DeSilva cousins were so jealous."

"And the bike was probably paid for by Gloria."

"Which doesn't make it right," Amber said. "Tell me about your eighth birthday."

"It was special." Mallory's turquoise eyes took on a gentle sheen and she smiled. "Mom took me and two of my friends for a ride in a hot-air balloon."

"Compare an idyllic balloon ride floating through the clouds with a messy party, surrounded by cousins and family while Felix snapped photos. Doesn't feel special, does it?" She pushed the box of letters away from herself. "I would have traded a dozen bikes for the chance to spend actual physical time with the woman who gave birth to me."

"It's not too late," Mallory said. "You could still have a relationship."

"Don't give a damn about Ingrid or Gloria or whatever she's calling herself this week. All I want is my share of the payoff. I never want to see her or hear from her."

Before Mallory could pipe up with another defense of her beloved Gloria, Shane stopped their argument. "I want to know more about Felix Komenda. Those first letters indicate that he's in Colorado. Amber, has he contacted you?"

"No, and I tried his phone and sent a text. He didn't answer."

"Does Mallory have his number?"

"I do," she said. "When Felix came to Aspen to discuss the sales of his artwork, he usually moved into Mom's extra bedroom. Once, he stayed at the Hotel Jerome. I'll check there and find out if he's registered. In the meantime, we can go to Reflections and look for more clues."

"Seems like a huge waste of time for all of us to poke around at the gallery," Amber said. "Felix used to talk about the gemology exhibit at the Museum of Nature and Science in Denver. I could go into the city and talk to the guy in charge."

"Ty Rivera," Mallory said. "One of Felix's letters mentioned him."

Shane loved the idea of sending Amber off on a quest of her own. "It's a plan," he said. "We'll take you to Reflections where you can pick up your rental car. You go to Denver, and we'll talk to each other tonight to compare notes."

"Can I trust you?" Amber scowled. "If you people stumble across the Teardrop, why would you contact me?"

"Because you're my sister, and I want the best for you."

For a moment, both were smiling. But Shane didn't believe the hostilities were over. They'd had twenty-six years of separation, and that distance wouldn't be erased in one day. Still, he was willing to accept this temporary truce between the two sisters.

Chapter Nine

After they wolfed down a quick but hearty lunch at Uncle Walter's place, Mallory and Shane dropped Amber off at her rented SUV outside Reflections. While he helped her clear the accumulated snow off her vehicle and Elvis dashed around the uncleared parking lot in lopsided figure eights, Mallory sat back in the passenger seat and put through one of the phone calls suggested by Uncle Walter.

Though she'd expected to get the nurse/receptionist Olivia or a recorded message, a familiar male voice answered on the third ring. "Dr. Freestone here."

"Hi, Doc." She'd known him literally since the day she was born, and he always made her smile. "How about this snow?"

"I'm looking forward to hitting the slopes, but the storm played havoc with my schedule. Olivia didn't make it in, and all my morning appointments canceled. Have you heard anything about your mother?"

"I know she was in Brooklyn three days ago."

"New York, eh? She didn't tell you she was going there?"

"She left a note. All it said was, I'll be back."

"Erratic behavior." He hummed to himself. "Even for Gloria, it's erratic."

"That's why I'm calling," she said. "Walter Pulaski suggested that you might know something about her state of mind. Is she sick? Does she have amnesia? Maybe she mentioned travel or visiting a friend."

"State of mind, yes." He hummed some more, and she could almost see him tapping his pencil to the tuneless beat. Freestone fancied himself a musician and had played in a band of nurses and interns called The Infarction in the '80s. "I really can't talk about her medical issues. Patient-doctor confidentiality, you know."

"Of course."

"But I wonder if Gloria had ever spoken to you about, um, you know. About the change?"

"What change?"

"I'm talking about menopause. Some women her age start thinking of rejuvenation and plastic surgery. Maybe breast augmentation. Maybe she'd considered expanding to a D-cup."

Mallory's jaw dropped. *Mom had gone shopping for a boob job, what?* Had she run off to New York to find a specialist plastic surgeon? "Can't believe it."

"In my experience, women who seek augmentation…" He picked up with his humming again. "Well, they often have a new boyfriend."

She stumbled through the rest of their conversation and thanked Dr. Freestone for his insights before she ended the call. Looking through the windshield, she saw that Shane was done helping Amber and making sure her rental car started. Mist from breathing in the cold surrounded him as he returned to the Navigator. He opened the rear door for Elvis and got behind the wheel. "I'll park in that stand of pines around back. The trees will camouflage the car, and nobody will get the idea that Reflections is open."

When she dropped her hand onto his parka above the wrist, the light dusting of snow melted against her flesh. The cold braced her. No matter how confused she was by Amber's hostility and Gloria's erratic behavior, Mallory couldn't allow herself to go numb. She had to keep her head in the game. "New theory," she said. "Dr. Freestone suggested it."

"Okay."

"Mom took off because she has a new boyfriend."

He started the engine. "That's a hell of a theory. Her disappearance and the search involving every rescue team in Pitkin County is because of a guy she's romancing?"

"The Doc told me Gloria was thinking about having a boob job. In his mind, that particular surgery equals boyfriend. Maybe she'll turn up in a couple of days with a new body and ask why we were worried."

Though they needed to consider every possibility, she doubted this scenario. Gloria was famous for her positive body image, didn't mind disrobing to pose as an artist's model. Uncle Walter had sculpted her nude from dozens of angles.

"There's a quick way to eighty-six that theory," he said as he drove to the back entrance of Reflections. "The Aspen police obtained her phone records. I'll check with them and find out if she's been calling plastic surgeons."

"And Hooker, the pawnbroker in Brooklyn. See if she talked to him."

He snugged the Navigator among the pine trees and turned toward her. "When we get inside, I want you to lead me through the search. Think like Gloria. Don't waste time running around and peeking in obscure corners."

"This won't be the first time I've searched Reflections."

"But now you're looking for a diamond that can be hidden in a small space."

"Got it." She noticed that he already had his door partially open. "Are we in a hurry?"

"Let's just say that I trust Amber about as much as she trusts us, which is not at all. She might be working with Burdock. If she locates the diamond, I doubt she'll share with us. I hope we find the jewel before she does."

She nodded. "I'm ready."

"After we're done here, our investigation will move to my cabin where I can make phone calls and launch computer searches. More crimes are solved by research than by action." He shrugged. "My dad told me that."

"Then you'd better listen."

He shot her a quizzical look. "Why would you say that?"

"I did some research of my own after I hired you."

"And what did you find out?"

"Enough." She'd learned that his father and brother, who he casually referred to as cops, were high-ranking officers in the DPD. His father was a deputy chief with half a dozen commendations including a Medal of Honor, and his brother was a sergeant in the Major Crimes Division. Needless to say, his family wouldn't get along with Gloria. Not a topic she wanted to delve into.

Inside the kitchen at Reflections, she was struck by the faint lingering scent of fresh baked goods: breads, muffins, cinnamon coffee cake and rolls. A shame to let this food go to waste. She put in a call to Sylvia Harrison and arranged for her and her cowboy husband to come over and take the food—as well as anything else perishable—to someone who could use it.

"What's going on?" Sylvia asked.

"Shane and I might have to go into Denver for a few days. I want to leave Reflections locked up tight with the alarm system set. We'll be closed for at least three or four days."

"Don't worry. I'll come by tonight to pick up the baked goods. Over the next few days, I'll check on things."

"Bring your big strong cowboy husband with you." If anything bad happened to Sylvia, Mallory would never forgive herself. "No risks. Understand?"

"I know it's dangerous. Don't you remember? I was the one who found the puddle of blood on the kitchen floor."

And she must have mopped it up because the kitchen was clean and clutter cleaned away. Mallory was lucky to have such a smart efficient person as her second-in-command. After she ended the call, she glanced around the large room with high windows and tried to decide if Gloria would have hidden anything in here. Not likely. There was a distinct lack of privacy. Too many others—employees and delivery people and suppliers—came and went.

Skirting the area on the kitchen floor where she imagined the blood had pooled, she strode through the swinging door into the coffee shop. Shane stood at the cantilevered window, gazing out at the gentle snowfall on the sculpture garden. He'd shed his parka, and his thermal turtleneck and vest outlined his muscular upper body and wide shoulders. His sun-streaked brown hair fell across his forehead in rumpled waves. He was as handsome as the artworks in the gallery. Plus, Shane had the added advantage of being warm-blooded and mobile. When he turned to face her, a spark of electricity zipped through the air and struck her nerve endings like a lightning bolt. Paralyzed, she continued to stare.

Elvis padded toward her and nudged her thigh. When she glanced down, she noticed the dog looking up with eyebrows raised. Never before had she seen a dog roll his eyes, but Elvis managed to convey a nonverbal urging for her to "get it together."

Shane came closer, moving as confidently and smoothly across the travertine tiles as when he whooshed down a ski slope on his way to an Olympic medal. When he was near enough, his golden-brown eyes linked with hers, and the electricity accelerated to a high-intensity whirr. She saw his lips move but couldn't make sense of the words. "What?"

"Let's get started," he repeated.

The sooner they launched into this search, the sooner they'd be finished. Then they'd drive to his cabin where they'd spend the night. Just the two of them, with him guarding her body. They'd be alone, except for the smart aleck dog.

SHANE APPRECIATED THE clever use of space in the gallery. Gloria might be an irredeemable wing nut, but she showed a touch of brilliance in the way she curated art. The walls and partitions on the main display floor kept to neutral tones—soft white, cool gray and beige—to avoid clashing with the paintings. The arrangement of partitions with wide-open areas and sharp corners felt like a labyrinth drawing him deeper into the array of passionate oil paintings, airy watercolors and intense abstracts. Around random corners, sculptures of all sizes and shapes were lurking.

He trailed behind Mallory as she wove through the displays, pointing out the way artists were grouped with several of their paintings together. "On the lower level, we have storage for more of their work. If a patron shows serious interest, we might take them down to the cellar for a more in-depth display of the artist's work."

He paused in front of a huge oil painting of a sunset, five by seven feet. Beside it were two smaller paintings of dawn and high noon. "Tell me about these."

"The artist is local. He only paints sky." She stood in front of the sunset and took a few steps back for a better perspective. "Makes sense, I guess. He's a pilot, Steve Fordham."

"Does he have a private plane?"

"He has several, the Fordham Fleet. Two choppers, three little Cessnas and a midsize executive jet. I think it's a Gulfstream."

"The sort of aircraft that could easily make a flight to Brooklyn."

When she whirled around to face him, her long blond braid flipped over her shoulder. "You think Gloria convinced him to take her to New York. But why wouldn't he tell me? Everybody in Aspen knows I'm looking for her."

Offhand, he could think of several reasons. The guy might still be in New York. Or Gloria could have convinced him that it was a secret. Or he could be in love with her. Maybe he was the new boyfriend. "Put him on your list of people to call. Catching a private flight would explain why her name never showed up on a passenger manifest."

She leaned forward and pulled an orange sticky note from a wall plaque with the name of the artist and the artwork. She held it for him to see Gloria's familiar scrawl.

He read the words. "Out of kombucha."

"It's a health drink. Gloria's latest craze."

"Does she leave many of these notes to herself?"

"All the time. She carries a pad of stickies in her pocket." Mallory exhaled an exasperated sigh, probably thinking of the cryptic note her mother had dropped before she disappeared. "I don't think she'd give directions to the Teardrop in a sticky note, but we should probably try to read most of them."

Once he'd become aware of the notes, he saw them everywhere. The messages ranged from trivial reminders to pick up the dry cleaning to scribbled phone numbers to dinner invitations. Disconnected pieces of Gloria were scattered throughout the gallery. Nothing pertained to the African Teardrop. As far as he could tell, there were no hints about the location of the gem. In the far corner of the gallery, he reached for the doorknob on an office.

"Don't bother," Mallory said. "I've gone over both offices with a fine-toothed comb. Those were the first place I searched."

"You're sure?"

"Absolutely."

She led the way to a circular metal staircase, and he followed. While she lectured about the addition of this narrow loft that was twelve feet above the floor of the main gallery and ten feet down from the open beam ceiling, his gaze slid lower on her body. He focused on the swell of her hips and her delicious, round bottom. Her jeans were a perfect fit. The Vibram soles of her hiking boots clunked on the metal steps, and yet her ascent flowed gracefully. Mallory in motion was a sight to behold.

The displays in the long narrow space beside the wall were small paintings, individually lit, and cases of original jewelry—mostly silver and turquoise—which Mallory studied carefully, peering into corners to find the diamond. He didn't follow her gaze. Instead, his attention riveted to her. He watched every gesture and the way her arms moved. Her slender throat. The tilt of her head when she glanced over her shoulder to make eye contact.

Shane forced himself to look away so he could sever this connection and end his fascination with her body. He rested his elbows on the iron railing at the edge of the loft and gazed down into the displays. Though there wasn't anything in the PI rule book forbidding him from hitting on a client, he knew it would be inappropriate. *Even though she'd kissed me first.* He needed to concentrate on his job, namely finding Gloria.

Mallory joined him at the railing, and he felt her warmth, heard the gentle whisper of her breathing and smelled the citrus scent of her shampoo. Instead of looking at her and being sucked into fantasy again, he gestured wide to encompass the displays on the floor below them. "Someday in the far distant future, all this will be yours."

"The gallery is Mom's passion. Not mine. Don't get me wrong, I love Reflections. But running a gallery isn't my dream."

"Tell me what is."

"I'll show you."

She pivoted and stalked the length of the loft to the metal staircase. Descending, he didn't have the distraction of watching her hips. Instead, he gazed at the swing of her braid and imagined unfastening that gleaming plait, strand by strand.

At the opposite end of the gallery, she paused outside a closed door beside the coffee shop. "When Mom bought this place, it was a fully functioning restaurant with a huge wine cellar in the basement. We transformed that space into storage for artwork."

He nodded. "You mentioned that some of the artists on display had other pieces for special clients' viewing."

"And the former wine cellar can be kept at sixty-five degrees with a humidity level of forty-eight percent. Perfect for maintaining the art in prime condition."

He doubted that primo storage conditions had anything to do with Mallory's dreams. "What else is down there?"

She pushed open the basement door and led him down into her lair. "This is my part of Reflections, which is why I don't think Mom would hide her treasure down here. The idea just wouldn't occur to her."

Subtle but well-placed lighting illuminated a long room with thick colorful rugs on the carpeted floor. Beanbag chairs mingled with regular seating and tables. The chalkboard had lettering in various hues. Corkboards in a rainbow array of frames, ranging from violet to red, decorated the walls and were filled with lively, imaginative paintings.

He'd seen a similar display at her house and drew the obvious conclusion. "These are from your students."

"Yes."

"You want to be a teacher."

"Yes."

Her dream seemed readily attainable, but he didn't make the mistake of thinking her ambitions were easy. Obstacles arose when you least expected them. He knew from experience that when everything seemed to be going well, disaster could strike.

Chapter Ten

By the time they left Reflections, the sun had begun to dip behind the low-hanging remnants of snow clouds. Roads were mostly cleared, and people were out and about, celebrating the first decent snowfall of the winter season. Mallory gazed through the windshield at the winding road that climbed the rugged hills above the Roaring Fork Valley.

Today's intense concentration on Gloria had been exhausting, and she set aside her fear, frustration and confusion. Instead, she thought about Shane. She'd never been to his cabin and didn't know what to expect. During his pro-skiing years, he must have been raking in the dough from prize money, endorsements and private lessons. He'd been famous for hosting extreme, off-piste skiing trips for wealthy clients. Did he squirrel away every penny? Or spend lavishly on a mountain mansion? Was he modern or traditional? Fancy or rustic? They'd spent a lot of time together, but she didn't really *know* him.

She needed to *know*. They'd be spending the night together and *anything* could happen. Her instincts urged her to take their simmering attraction to the next level, but she needed to figure out what to expect from him on the morning after. A cynical, clinical way of forming an opinion about sex, but she'd been hurt too many times to risk her heart.

After years of dating, she'd come up with guidelines to decide potential compatibility. Her categories for bachelor pads ranged from "elite," which was decorator glam with every detail perfect, to "slob" for apartments with empty pizza boxes as the predominant decor. Elite guys usually picked her apart and found her lacking. Slobs were too cluttered to think of anything but themselves. She hoped Shane fell somewhere in between.

Nearing his home, she checked out the view. *Spectacular.* His property stretched along the edge of a cliff, overlooking a scenic snow-covered valley with snow-capped peaks in the distance. His cabin—twice as large as her house—had log siding, a peaked roof over a covered porch, a partial second floor and a tall stone chimney. Classy but not pretentious.

Was he secretly a slob? Or, equally problematic, obsessively tidy? As he guided the Navigator into a neatly shoveled driveway leading to a three-car garage, she asked, "Did you clear the snow this morning before you left?"

"I've got a guy who shovels in the winter, rakes in the fall and mows in the summer. I hired him when I got back from rehab and all my physical energy needed to go into therapy."

"But you're recovered now."

"It's a luxury," he admitted. "But he's worth it. I've also got a twice-a-month cleaning person and an office assistant who I call when necessary."

He scored another plus by recognizing that sometimes he needed help. Also, she liked the responsible way he took care of the things he owned and didn't have a full-time housekeeper to fuss over him. *Not an entitled rich guy.*

The interior of his extra-large garage was well lit with shelving across the back wall. He parked in the slot nearest the entry to his house. A Ford truck—older model, beat-up but clean—was next to that. The rest of the space was filled with sporting equipment, including an ATV. Not surprising. She'd known from the moment she met him that Shane was the athletic type, which suited her just fine. Mallory loved mountain sports. Hitting the slopes in winter. Rock climbing and kayaking in summer. Jogging year-round.

Before they left the garage, he reset the digital alarm. "This system is separate from the interior of the house. If you come in here, you've got thirty seconds to disarm it."

"Then what happens?"

"A screaming alarm and a security firm is alerted. They call. If I don't give them the correct password, they'll be here inside of fifteen minutes."

He didn't sound paranoid, but still she wondered. "Why separate systems?"

"Some of the equipment in the garage is valuable."

Shane slung the giant backpack over his shoulder and scooped up the box of letters from Felix. In the mudroom behind the kitchen, he hung his parka and stomped the last bit of snow off his boots. She did the same. Elvis scooted past them, and she followed the dog into an efficient-looking kitchen with hardwood floors, walnut cabinets and black granite countertops. Elvis trotted past a circular breakfast table and proceeded directly to his water bowl in front of the sliding glass door leading onto a snow-covered deck. Through the windows, a red and gold sunset streaked the sky.

Elvis nudged her thigh. When she looked down at him, he sashayed over to his water bowl and tapped the empty food dish beside it. "I understand," she said. "You're hungry."

He gave her an Elvis-like sneer and used his snout to push the food dish toward her.

She called to Shane. "I think your dog is trying to tell me that he's starving."

Shane joined her, shot a glance at Elvis and shook his head. "You ain't nothing but a hound dog, but I'll get your kibble."

"What about you and me?" she asked. "What should we do for dinner?"

She'd already had plenty of opportunity to watch him eat and knew that he preferred healthy options. But a gander inside his shiny double-door refrigerator would tell her if he was gourmet curious or solid meat-and-potatoes.

While he filled the dog's bowl, he asked, "What can I get you to drink? Coffee or tea? Wine or something stronger?"

"Water is fine."

"I've got fizzy and flat, but I usually drink whatever comes out of the tap. One of the reasons I bought this house was the excellent well water."

He earned a double thumbs-up from her. Real mountain people were concerned first and foremost about their water situation. "Tap water sounds great."

"For dinner, I'm thinking honey-glazed pork chops with acorn squash and a balsamic reduction on a caprese salad."

A menu that sounded both delicious and fascinating. *Like him?* "Do you do your own cooking?"

"I got into the habit after my accident. Before then, I never had time. Now, making dinner is how I unwind. I come in here, turn on some music, call up a recipe online and cook."

Music was another area for consideration. Mallory was open to many different styles but definitely had favorites. "What do you listen to?"

"Depends on what I'm doing. I like a heavy beat when I'm running or exercising."

"Are you a country-western fan? Do you prefer classical?"

"Both." He took two glasses down from the shelf beside the sink and confronted her with a steady gaze. "You're asking a lot of questions."

"Just curious."

"Ever since we met, you've been focused on Gloria. Now you've turned the spotlight on me." He turned on the tap and filled the glasses. "What's going on?"

"You're very perceptive." Another point in his favor. But she didn't want to tell him that she'd been judging him. "Have you ever been in therapy?"

"All kinds of therapy. Physical and psychological. And I went to a psychic once."

"You have an open mind. That's good." She took the water glass and swallowed a couple of long gulps. Maybe she ought to abandon her questions. She liked him and vice versa. Shouldn't that be enough to decide where their relationship went? Still, she wasn't sure what skeletons he had in his closet. "Aren't you going to show me around your house?"

He escorted her through the living room, furnished with comfortable modern furniture in shades of blue and gold. The stone fireplace held a long mantel where he'd chosen to display framed photos, Navajo pottery and geodes. He showed her a picture of two kids, a boy and girl. "My nephew and niece. He's seven, and she's five."

"Your brother's children." The warmth in his voice told her that he liked kids. *Another plus.* "How long has he been married?"

"Almost ten years. Cops are famous for having difficult relationships. But not Logan. He and Cheryl are still crazy about each other. They keep trying to fix me up with the perfect mate."

This was a big topic. *Huge.* "Have you been married before?"

"I've come close. Had a couple of long-term relationships, but nothing worked out. In the early years of my career, I was too preoccupied with skiing. After the accident, I had to rebuild myself before I dragged someone else into my messed-up life."

Though she was curious, probing into his breakups was too nosy, even for her. She gestured to the mantel. "I expected to see trophies. Where do you keep your Olympic medal?"

"Another question." He ducked into the kitchen, retrieved her giant backpack and strode down the hallway. Gesturing to an open door, he said, "This is my office."

She peeked inside. The large space held a desk, file cabinets and a long sofa behind a coffee table. The bronze third-place medal in giant slalom hung in a frame on the wall beside a photo of Shane and the rest of the US team in their uniforms. The placement told her that he wasn't egotistical about his win but treated the accomplishment with respect. *Perfect.*

He went down the hall to a bedroom. After placing her pack on an antique-looking steamer chest at the foot of the queen-size bed, he turned to face her. "I usually sleep upstairs but I'm moving down here for the night. I'll be right across the hall."

"You're taking the bodyguard thing seriously."

"Hell, yes." He stepped back into the hall. "We'll be sharing a bathroom."

In addition to the sink, toilet and shower, the outer wall of the pearl-tiled room held a whirlpool bath that was eight feet long. Her analysis of Shane came to a screeching halt as she perched at the edge of the tub. Any guy who owned a whirlpool with twelve—she counted them—jets went to the head of the line. "Loving it."

"The controls are over here. The jets have two different actions. And this one is for a chromotherapy function that turns on pastel lights."

"Water churning. And lights, too?" Better than a ride at the amusement park.

He leaned against the tiled wall. "About all those questions. What's the deal?"

"Do you really want to know?"

"That's why I asked."

"You've been around me long enough to understand a few things about Mom and the way I was raised." She glided her fingertips along the high-gloss white acrylic of the tub. "Gloria didn't give me many rules. She always said if it feels good, do it. I had to make my own decisions and come up with my own boundaries."

"Okay, but I need more explanation."

"When I get interested in a man, I have a series of questions that tell me if he's a good bet for a relationship."

"You've been testing me?"

"In a way."

The easygoing grin fell from his face, and the light in his caramel-colored eyes faded. The temperature in the bathroom dropped by several degrees. "What's the decision, Mallory? Am I good enough for you?"

"When you say it like that, my perfectly rational process sounds creepy."

"You bet it does." He pushed away from the wall and headed for the bathroom door. "Dinner will be ready in an hour and a half."

BEFORE HE GOT started in the kitchen, Shane grabbed the box of letters, went to his office accompanied by Elvis and closed the door. Didn't slam it, though he wanted to. He dropped the box by the couch, then flung himself into the ergonomic swivel chair behind the desk—a chair which Mallory would probably disapprove of because the design with special back support had cost a bundle. She'd think he wasn't practical. And where did she get off judging him? Why did he have to justify himself? Prove himself worthy? He glanced down at Elvis who rested his head on Shane's knee and waited for a pet.

"Why do I care?" He scratched behind the Lab's velvety ears. "She's a client. It ought to be enough that she's paying me for my time."

He wondered if dogs had the same kind of problem with mating. Did Elvis ever approach a female in heat who rejected him? Probably had. Sooner or later, some hot poodle would turn up her nose at him. Just like a bitch.

That description didn't apply to Mallory. She was different. At least, he'd thought so. Sure, she looked like a typical Colorado blonde with long straight hair, a sun-kissed complexion and a tight athletic body, but she lacked the snotty attitude that usually accompanied that natural beauty. Mallory seemed sweet, hardworking, considerate and genuinely concerned about others. He'd wanted to protect her. Not only from physical danger but from the slings and arrows of gossip. Growing up with someone like her mother must have been a challenge, which still didn't justify her system of making a list of requirements for her friends and lovers. He paused. Had she been considering him for the latter role?

A lover, her lover? Shane felt himself smiling through his anger. Most certainly, he'd been looking at her that way. Was she on the same page? *This had to stop. Now.* He had to quit mooning over Mallory and get down to the business of being a competent private eye. "That's right, Elvis. Isn't it?"

The Lab bobbed his head, which meant he either agreed or he wanted more pets.

Shane rose from his comfortable desk chair and went to the leather sofa by the wall and sat beside the box of letters from Felix. Logic told him that somewhere in that stack of memories was a clue. At random, he pulled out a brown envelope and sorted through the contents, noting Felix's excellent penmanship and his attention to detail. He had described Amber's birthday party dress with incredible clarity. He chatted about weather, writing vivid descriptions of the skies over Manhattan and the foliage in Central Park. When it came to clues, nothing jumped out.

Though not really hungry, Shane needed to get started

with dinner. There would definitely be wine, something to take the edge off. Later tonight, he'd check in with his brother and launch into computer research into Gloria's possible aliases. If she'd used a credit card, he could analyze where she'd gone and what she was doing.

For now, his only reference points came from these old letters. Felix had mentioned Ty Rivera in the gemology displays at the Museum of Nature and Science in Denver. And there were references to other friends who Gloria might contact. He and Mallory might need to take a trip into the city.

Shoving the letters back in their envelopes, he rose from the sofa, stretched his arms over his head and yawned. As long as he concentrated on detective work, he could avoid thinking about Mallory in a more intimate, personal, delectable way. Just a client, she was only a client. No matter how much he wanted to run his fingers through her silky hair and carry her into his bedroom, that wasn't part of their bargain. All he owed her were answers about her mother.

Chapter Eleven

When she took her place at the table, Mallory inhaled the rich aroma of perfectly grilled chops and vinaigrette. The stoneware plates were caramel and slate blue. Stemmed wineglasses held an enticing splash of ruby pinot noir. Streaming music in the background featured lovable divas, like Adele, Lady Gaga and Elton John. A perfect dinner, except for one thing. Shane's mood was stiffly polite, almost cold.

She hadn't meant to make him angry, but that was the end result of her questioning and judging. Did that mean he was too proud or too sensitive? Or was it a reflection on her? The first time she'd met him, she'd been attracted. Who wouldn't be? He was a handsome, athletic man with a good sense of humor who talked to his dog. *Adorable*.

But she had to be cautious when it came to relationships. The therapist she'd gone to for a while suggested that because she'd never known her father, she had subconscious daddy issues that made her crave attention from men. Whatever the reason, she often fell too hard, too fast.

She couldn't stand to be hurt again. And so, she accepted the awkward silence that fell between them, making his cozy dining area seem as dismal as a dungeon.

After dinner, Shane retired to his office to do computer research on Gloria. Mallory also had phone calls to make, but she insisted on cleaning up the dishes, which only seemed fair because he'd cooked. While she tidied the countertops, rinsed and stacked the plates in the dishwasher, Elvis kept her company. The black Lab's attentive gaze encouraged conversation, and she said, "I hope Shane doesn't stay mad."

Elvis gave a snort.

"Yeah, I deserve it. I should have thought of how insulting it was before interrogating him. Is it really such a big deal? People judge each other all the time. It makes sense to base decisions about relationships on past experiences."

When the dishes were done, Elvis followed her down the hallway to her bedroom where she grabbed her basic toiletries and a long flannel nightgown. Hoping to sweep the broken fantasies about Shane from her mind, she ducked into the gleaming white bathroom, started the hot water and found a fluffy blue bath towel that she placed within easy reach beside the tub. Before she disrobed, she scampered back to the kitchen and poured herself another glass of red wine, which she took to the bathroom. Elvis followed her inside.

With a barrette, she fastened her braid on top of her head, undressed and slid into the water. Steam rose in thick clouds that fogged the corner windows overlooking a cliff. No one could see inside unless they had the ability to hover like a helicopter. Even with all this glass, the bathroom wasn't cold. Shane had assured her that the panes were triple thick for good insulation, which also meant bulletproof.

Tapping buttons and turning dials on the control panel, she adjusted the high-pressure action on the jets, starting a swirling, churning motion around her legs and feet. With her upper arms resting on the smooth edge of the tub, she positioned her back against the jets and sighed contentedly as the water pummeled and massaged. Her muscles relaxed, releasing the tension she'd been carrying since Mom ran away.

The heat from the bath opened her pores, and the earthy red wine warmed her on the inside. She fiddled with the control panel, discovering that she could dim the overhead lights and then turn them off entirely. In the dark, she gazed through the windows into the snow-covered forest. Distant mountains framed a cloudy night sky sprinkled with stars. She sipped the wine and tried to forget her worries, but as soon as she erased one crisis, another arose, then another. *Stop thinking.* She programmed the lights to sequentially go through the colors of a spectrum from blue to green to yellow to red. The tub water changed from a deep magenta to purple. *More wine.* Her art classes of elementary school kids would love this whirlpool.

She heard a knock at the door and bolted upright in the tub, nearly sloshing the pinot noir into the pulsating light show. She pressed buttons on the control panel. In her confusion, she plunged the bathroom into total darkness.

"Mallory, do you mind if I come in?"

"Maybe later." She didn't want him to see her wallowing in the dark and sucking down wine. "Not right now."

"Don't worry." He sounded irritated. "I promise not to look."

As if I care about modesty. She couldn't figure out the controls. Another button sent the jets into high speed like the mythical zx threatening to swallow her whole. Water splashed out of the tub, and the room was still dark. "Just a minute."

Elvis tilted back his head and howled, which she supposed was better than having the dog burst into laughter.

"What's Elvis barking at? What's going on?" Shane asked. "I'm coming in."

The bathroom door cracked open, and light from the hallway spilled inside. She saw his tall silhouette. Still wearing jeans, he'd changed into a long-sleeved flannel shirt rolled up at the cuffs. Elvis trotted over to his master and sat, thumping his tail on the floor. The two of them exchanged a glance, then looked in her direction. She'd never felt so utterly, totally naked.

"Before you come any closer," she said, "I just want to tell you that I'm sorry for prying and judging and not trusting you."

"Can we turn on the lights? I won't peek."

"There's nothing shameful about the human body." She'd been posing in the nude for art classes since she was sixteen. "I didn't mean for it to be dark in here. I was hitting buttons and accidentally turned off the lights."

"It's kind of nice like this." He crossed the bathroom and approached the tub. "There's just enough moonlight from the window to outline the shape of your head and shoulders."

"Do you forgive me?"

"Oh, yeah." His husky voice soothed her fear that he'd despise her, but she was still tense. He hunkered down by the tub so he was eye level with her. "I can't stay mad at a water sprite, if that's what you are. More likely a wood nymph."

Or a wood nymphomaniac. His nearness combined with

the wine, churning water and her nudity set her hormones on fire. Looking away from him, she watched Elvis come closer with his toenails clicking on the tile floor. She gave the dog a fake scowl. "Now you're my friend, huh? After setting up a howl and making Shane think I was in trouble. You threw me under the bus."

The dog raised his eyebrows as if to say, "Who, me?"

"Yeah, you." She splashed him, and Elvis stepped back.

"Hey, don't take out your frustration on the dog."

She aimed a second splash at Shane. "Who says I'm frustrated?"

He wiped droplets of water from his cheek and forehead. In the glow of moonlight through the windows, he looked cool and calm, almost businesslike. As for Mallory? Not so much. She was nude and her pulse was racing—the opposite of unperturbed. "Why was it so important for you to come in here? Is there something you wanted to tell me?"

"I heard back from my brother and have information. Your mother has been using a credit card and identification from her youth when her name was Ingrid Stromberg."

"Whoa." *More wine.* "She went back in time."

"Ingrid Stromberg is a legitimate person. She has a bank account in Denver, files taxes and uses the credit card often enough to keep the account active, usually during her travels to New York and beyond."

"Why would she do that?" Mallory managed to dial the whirlpool jets back to a reasonable level. "What's the point?"

"A second identity can come in handy. Makes it easy to go incognito."

Which made her think that Mom had been planning all

along to disappear and start another new life by selling the Teardrop. Her work at Reflections was only a stopping point along the way and Mallory could be abandoned… like Amber. "What else?"

"She also has a cell phone in that name. My brother tracked the numbers she called and those who called her."

"Is anybody from Aspen on that list?" Mallory wanted to know if she'd been played for a fool. "How about Uncle Walter?"

"The only names I recognized were Ben Hooker, the fence, and Felix. I tried calling them both and leaving messages mentioning your name. Neither has returned my call."

"I almost hate to ask." A shudder wriggled down her backbone. "Has she been in contact with Conrad Burdock?"

"Her supposed enemy?" His fingertips dangled in the water, and she fought the urge to grab his hand and pull him into the tub with her. He continued, "Actually, he's the first name I looked for. We only have Amber's word that Burdock engineered the attack on Reflections, and I thought he might be one of your mom's phone contacts. But no."

"Can't your brother trace her whereabouts using her phone?"

He gave her a questioning look. "For somebody who doesn't want police involvement, you seem very willing to take advantage of their resources."

"Hey, I watch crime shows on TV. I know about tracking phone signals."

"Not as easy as it looks," he said. "My brother tried, but Gloria has a very old model and has either figured out a way to turn it off or she's thrown it away. There's been no activity on that phone since she got to New York."

Thanks to modern technology, they'd located her, but she'd slipped away before they could catch her. Mom had spent a lifetime evading notice and had gotten good at it. "What about travel? Did Ingrid Stromberg make plane reservations to New York?"

"He couldn't find any of her aliases on passenger manifests," Shane said. "I'm guessing she used her friend the pilot. What's his name again?"

"Steve Fordham."

"The good news," he said, "is that early this morning her credit card pinged at a restaurant in Denver. She's in Colorado. Didn't Amber say that she'd sent Hooker a photo of herself in Denver?"

"She did, and I guess I should call her with this new information." But it might not be wise to share with her sister. Though Mallory didn't want to imagine a conspiracy, it was possible that Gloria and Amber and Felix were working together and not telling her. If so, why would Amber contact her in the first place? "I'm confused. Too many secrets. Too many lies."

"I know."

"I should finish my bath and start driving to Denver."

"Not tonight. We're both tired. And we need a game plan."

"Smart. Logical." Denver was a four- to five-hour drive and a huge city. They couldn't just wander up and down every street calling her name. "I guess we need to do more research. Make a few more phone calls. Check the computer."

He pushed up his shirtsleeve, stretched his long arm

across the whirlpool to the control panel and adjusted the overhead lights to a dim glow. From his vantage point, he had a clear view of her naked body in the lightly swirling water, but she didn't care. In fact, she welcomed his gaze. They'd been ogling each other since the moment they met. It was time to take it to the next level. She was ready. Or was she?

She rested her forearms on the side of the tub and looked into Shane's eyes. Only inches from his face, she studied the pale brown, burnished gold and hazel facets of his iris beneath his dark brows. Light stubble shadowed his cheeks and emphasized the cleft in his chin.

Gently, he caressed her cheek and tucked a loose strand of hair behind her ear. Reaching up, he unhooked the barrette holding her long braid out of the water. The blond plait fell across her shoulder. "What are you doing?" she asked.

"Helping you unfasten your braid."

"Okay."

She swiveled around in the tub and sat with her back against the side while he took her braid in hand and gave a light tug. "Soft."

"Well, sure. It's hair."

"How long did it take to grow this length?"

"A while."

She covered her breasts with her palms, not because she was embarrassed but it seemed like a comfortable position. What else was she going to do with her hands? As he untwined her braid, she felt the length of it tickling her back and shoulders.

"I've got to admit," he said, "I'm kind of obsessed with your hair. It's mythic, like a mermaid."

"And what does that make you?"

"The hapless dope who can't resist your siren song."

She turned her head to face him. The whirlpool swirled around her legs, but he wouldn't let her float away from his grasp. Shane lifted her from the water and enclosed her in his arms. His kiss was liquid and sensual. His tongue slid between her teeth, exploring and then demanding. When she pressed her wet body against him, he rose to his feet, pulling her from the tub. Cool air raised goose bumps on her backside. He draped the fluffy blue towel around her shoulders.

"Wait," she said. "I have to wash my hair."

"Let me help. It'll be easier in the shower."

"Yes."

Though the distance from the tub to the shower was only a few feet, he guided her protectively across the white-tiled floor. Inside the glass enclosure, a rainfall showerhead splashed a steady flow upon her long hair. She turned her face up toward the hot water and allowed the rivulets to sluice down her throat and over her breasts. The dizzying effects of the wine lingered in a gentle buzz.

Then he was beside her in the shower, naked and muscular. She pushed the rising steam aside for a better view of his hard athletic body. He did not disappoint. Shane could have been one of Uncle Walter's sexy marble sculptures, except for the scars on his legs from his many surgeries after the skiing accident.

They soaped and rinsed and kissed. He paid particular attention to her hair, ending the shower by piling the long tresses under a towel on top of her head. After they dried off, he carried her—still naked—into the guest bedroom. When he tried to place her onto the comforter,

Elvis had already claimed the bed and sprawled posses-
sively across it.

Shane dropped her feet to the floor and shooed the dog.
"Sorry, buddy. Off the bed."

Elvis sneered and grumbled under his breath.

"You heard the boss," she said.

The dog hopped down and slouched out of the bedroom.
Shane closed the door behind him and turned to her. "Do
you really think I'm the boss?"

"Of the dog."

She threw aside the comforter and slid between the
dark blue sheets. He joined her and they embraced until
their damp flesh was warm. They made love throughout
the night.

THE NEXT MORNING, Mallory wakened slowly. She replayed
the night before, remembering one amazing climax after
another, crashing like waves against a distant shore. She
recalled a gentle moment when Shane had sung to her, and
she to him. Elvis had returned to the bedroom and joined
in. Happily exhausted, she'd slept.

Through the window, she saw blue skies. Elvis danced
between the bed and the bedroom door as if heralding the
arrival of breakfast. The aroma of fresh brewed coffee
rose from a large bed tray table where Shane had placed
two mugs and a plate of cinnamon rolls. His wide smile
emphasized his dimples. Oh, my god, he was handsome.

Before she could even say good morning, her phone
rang and she answered. The voice on the other end was
light and cheery. "Have you missed me?"

Mallory stared at her phone screen in disbelief. Caller
ID showed the name Hannah Wye, an attorney and a mid-

talent watercolor artist from Denver, but the voice definitely belonged to her mother. Mom's chuckle rippled through Mallory's memory, sparking the recall of a million jokes and sweet, silly games.

"What's the matter, honey pie?" Gloria asked. "Cat got your tongue?"

"Mom, where are you?"

"I'm so sorry if I upset you. It was never ever my intention to hurt you. You understand, don't you? That's why I left a note."

As she recalled the scribble, Mallory clenched her jaw. The note read, *I'll be back*.

"Mom, that's a tag line for a movie. Three damn words aren't an explanation for why you took off and disappeared for over a week without any other communication."

"A dear friend needed my help, and I simply couldn't say no to him."

"What friend?"

"Felix. You've met him. Tall, skinny, shaved head and tattoos up and down both arms. He's Black."

"Felix Komenda. Is he here in Colorado? Can I meet him?"

"Don't worry. Everything's going to be all right."

Just like that. Gloria expected the intense efforts of an all-out search to be forgiven. Never mind the risks and the long hours put in by the sheriff's office, Aspen police and Aspen/Pitkin County Search and Rescue teams. Mallory forced herself to remain calm. "Tell me where you are, and I'll pick you up."

"Not yet, munchkin. There's one more thing to do, then I'll come home."

"When?"

"Gotta run." Another musical chuckle. "When I get back, I'll answer all your questions."

"Will you? Will you, really?" Mallory had a lot more to say, but her throat choked up. She shoved the phone toward Shane.

He turned the volume up so she could hear, then he spoke into the screen. "May I ask a few questions?"

"Who the holy heck are you?"

"Shane Reilly. I'm a private investigator your daughter hired to locate you, Mrs. Greenfield."

"There's no need for further conversation. I was lost, but now I'm found. Like it says in the song." Her tone had changed. Mallory could tell that she was on the verge of an argument. "And I'm not a Mrs., for your information."

"Okay." Shane's shoulders tensed. "Would you prefer I call you by your maiden name? Or your prior married name? Ingrid DeSilva."

"How did you know?" Rage underlined her words. It went against her free-spirited, live-and-let-live attitude to get angry. But when she did, the effect was terrifying. "This is none of your damn business."

Mallory grabbed the phone. "Please don't hang up."

"How could you hire some creepy private eye to poke around in my life?"

"I was desperate, scared that you were hurt or even dead."

"I'd never die without letting you know."

"Please, Mom, tell me where you are."

"I'm so sorry, but I have to do this my way."

"Wait!"

"Goodbye, Mallory."

She couldn't let her go, couldn't let it end like this. "When were you planning to tell me about Amber? Did you fake your own death? Answer me, Mom. What happened to the priceless African Teardrop? Did you take it from your safe-deposit bank?"

The phone went dead.

Chapter Twelve

Gloria needed to put distance between herself and Hannah Wye's downtown Denver art studio/law office on Blake Street before her daughter and the private investigator sent someone to find her and drag her back to Aspen to face the consequences. Why were all these people getting in her way? She was trying to do the right thing, damn it. Ben Hooker in Brooklyn had turned out to be a Greedy Gus, which made her grateful that she hadn't brought the diamond with her to New York. Felix had been annoyingly uncooperative, and she could only hope that Ty Rivera at the museum would have better contacts. Then there was Mallory. How had her daughter discovered the theft of the Teardrop and how had she deduced that the diamond had been in her safe-deposit box at the bank? Worse, how had she learned about her sister?

Amber, dear little Amber. At the remembrance of the spunky blond child with turquoise eyes, an unexpected pain stabbed Gloria so hard that she doubled over. Her first baby, her darling Amber had been bright, athletic and strong. Even at four years old, she'd known her mind. Leaving Amber behind was the greatest regret of Gloria's life. She never could have done it if Felix hadn't been there to protect the child and keep her safe.

She stepped away from the landline phone, slung her backpack over her shoulder and stalked out the door, grateful that Hannah Wye had seen fit to give her a key of her own so she could pick up artwork even if the artist was out of town. Gloria hadn't been ready to return to Aspen last night, especially after she heard about several inches of snowfall in the mountains.

The city sidewalks had been spared from the storm. The air felt dry and relatively warm on this October morning. There was something good to be said for living at a lower elevation.

As she strolled past Coors Field and headed toward Larimer Square to the bistro where she'd meet with Felix for a breakfast of chai tea and muffins, Gloria remembered when she had lived at sea level. It had been twenty-six years ago...

AFTER SIX O'CLOCK, she had shuffled through the open-air marketplace of Freetown in Sierra Leone. The sunlight had begun to fade, and the night violence commenced. Tall modern buildings loomed over the colorful street where most of the stalls were vacant. The few people she saw shouted at her and told her to find safety. A futile warning.

The dangers of a civil war that had been ongoing since the early '90s seemed distant compared to the daily threat of living with her husband, Raymond DeSilva. Whenever his diamond-brokering business took them to Sierra Leone, he drank Jameson like it was water. And he blamed her for every little thing that went wrong. Even now, when she was seven months pregnant, he lashed out.

Thinking of his latest assault, she stumbled in her ill-fitting leather sandals. Raymond had shoved her to the floor, bruising her knees. That dull ache was nothing compared to the throbbing pain in her left wrist from when he'd twisted her arm and demanded that she admit to mishandling a computer entry about their inventory.

To end the pain, she admitted to a wrong she'd never committed and decided, at the same time, to leave the abusive monster. His violent attacks came more and more frequently. And he'd started drinking when they were home in Manhattan where Amber was being cared for by Raymond's parents. The thought of her daughter spiked tears. She hadn't asked to be dragged into this life, watching her father inflict painful punishment on her mother, hearing her mother's sobs. True enough, Raymond adored the child. His love for Amber was the only reason she'd stayed with him during these long painful years. She'd endure anything, absolutely anything, to be certain that Amber was protected.

Her long dress in a bold pattern of dark green, orange, yellow and brown flowed over her pregnant belly and brushed the pavement. Her long blond hair was piled on top of her head and wrapped in a yellow-and-green-striped turban. In spite of the tropical heat, she pulled a shawl around her shoulders, trying to become invisible and unnoticed. She wished she could disappear. Not for the first time, she wished she was dead.

At the end of the street, she saw a dozen young men with rifles. They shouted wildly and fired into the air. If she stood right here and faced them, she might be killed. Her nightmare would be over.

But that was not to be. Her friend Felix emerged from an alley, caught hold of her uninjured wrist and guided her away from the crossfire on the street. In his soothing accented voice, he said, "Come with me. This shall not be the end of you."

"I can't stay with him." She staggered down the narrow alley between sunbaked brick and stucco walls. When she protectively cradled her belly, pain knifed from her wrist down to the tips of her fingers and up to her elbow. "I can't bring another child into this hell."

"Divorce him."

A bitter laugh fell from her lips. Raymond would never agree to a divorce, and not because he loved her. "He'd rather kill me than pay alimony or child support."

"Your husband has enemies. They seek to destroy him."

According to Raymond, the aura of hatred surrounding him was her fault. Though she sat quietly in a corner and said not a word, she had offended people and turned them against him. "Felix, do people hate me?"

"Not at all."

"But I don't have friends."

"My country is at war. Friendship is a luxury few can afford."

He was a kind man, the only person she trusted. And she believed him when he told her about the plans of Raymond's enemies. They intended to set off a bomb in the dingy two-story office building where DeSilva Gems kept a small office in Freetown.

She knew they were close to the plain ugly building with bars on the windows and double locks on every door. They needed to go there, to warn her husband. She hated Raymond but wasn't a murderer.

"He is not there," Felix said. "He does not work late."

She knew as much. She knew he was at their rented apartment where she'd left him with his half-empty bottle of whiskey. He'd ordered her to go out into the streets where she was supposed to go to the office and pick up one of the ledgers. Her husband had sent her directly into the line of fire.

In the destructive orange flare of multiple explosions on the streets of Freetown, she saw her future. The cries of victims and attackers urged her forward. This was her chance to run.

If she could clean out Raymond's diamond inventory before the building was destroyed, she'd be presumed dead in the explosion. There would be no reason to come after her, to chase a ghost. With the sale of the precious gems, she could finance her escape from Africa.

Raymond wouldn't care that she was gone. Insurance would cover his loss from the stolen gems. And she would disappear into a new life of freedom and safety…and heart-wrenching sorrow. She would have to leave her beloved Amber behind.

Chapter Thirteen

Shane approached Mallory carefully. Fragile as a porcelain statue, she sat motionless in the center of the bed with her legs tucked beneath her and her head drooping forward. A curtain of straight blond hair hid her face. Still naked, she clutched the dark blue sheet over her breasts and shivered. But when she lifted her chin, he didn't see tears. Though the call from Gloria had obviously left her shaken, her eyes remained dry. How could a mother treat her child with such callous disregard? So wrong, so very wrong.

Carefully, he moved the tray with two mugs of coffee off the bed and placed it on the floor. Then he reached for her cell phone. From the corner of his eye, he saw Elvis sneaking toward the tray and warned him off. "Don't even think about eating those cinnamon rolls."

The dog sneered.

"I mean it," Shane snapped. He didn't have time for games. "Don't touch. Step away from the breakfast pastries."

With a shrug, the dog obeyed. Shane joined Mallory on the bed and glided his arm around her. She melted into his embrace and exhaled a sigh. "I shouldn't be surprised by Mom's refusal to talk to me. Everybody has secrets."

No wonder she didn't give her trust easily. Her father

couldn't be counted on; he'd never been around. Her sister was hostile, cold and completely out for herself. As for her mother? Her mom's whole life was a lie. He wasn't inclined to let Gloria get away with this. If she didn't face the illegality of her actions, she should at least acknowledge the damage done to her children. He whispered, "We'll find her."

"Yeah, sure." She nuzzled her head under his chin. "Please don't tell me everything is going to be all right. I can't take another lie."

"No promises, but I'll do whatever I can."

She tilted her head back and looked into his eyes. The line of her cheekbone and chin formed a delicate silhouette. "We need to get moving," she said. "And that's kind of a shame."

"Why?"

"Another disappointment. Like the fact that you're completely dressed. You know, I'd hoped we'd have some time this morning...time for us."

"I'm glad you feel that way." Last night had been outstanding, both in the shower and in the bed. Did he want more? Hell, yes. But they had to wait. He dropped a light kiss on her forehead and on the tip of her nose. "Before we go, there's something we need to do."

"Something fun?"

"Something necessary." He picked up her phone. "We need to turn this thing off and take out the battery."

"But you already made the signal untraceable."

"This is an extra precaution."

"Just let me call Sylvia and check on Reflections." She clutched the phone to her breast. "Then you can turn it off."

"Don't forget. Those guys in ski masks who chased after us in the Hummer worry me." He stroked her silky hair. "I don't want them to be able to find you. So, call Sylvia and hand over your phone. We'll have our coffee and get rolling."

When he reached down to pick up the bed tray, he saw that the coffee mugs were undisturbed but the pastries were gone, and Elvis had smears of frosting on his nose. "Bad dog."

"What did he do?"

"Ate the cinnamon rolls, didn't you?" The Lab ducked his head. His brow wrinkled, and he looked totally ashamed. "Oh, man, I can't believe you."

When she leaned forward, the sheet slipped lower and gave him an even more enticing view. She reached toward the dog who crawled toward her, rested his chin on the bed and whimpered. "It's okay, sweetie. Shane's being mean."

"I can't let him get away with stuff like this." And he couldn't indulge her by allowing her to keep her phone. His job was to protect both of them. "It's not good for him to eat sugary stuff, especially rolls with raisins."

"Then you shouldn't have left the cinnamon rolls so close. You can't blame Elvis for giving in to temptation."

Shane handed her the coffee mug. "Have some caffeine."

"You're right. We have to get going. It's a long drive to Denver."

"Who said anything about driving?"

She cocked her eyebrows. "What did you have in mind?"

"I know a guy," he said. "We used to work together when I took rich tourists on extreme skiing excursions to remote terrain. Long story short, he'd drop us off in the backcountry."

"By helicopter?"

"We're supposed to meet him at nine thirty, which means we've got to hurry. I've already contacted SAR to let them know I'll be out of town. And my answering service."

He left her to get dressed and drink her coffee while he dashed upstairs to his primary suite, grabbed a dark blue cashmere sweater from his closet and pulled it over his button-down shirt and khakis. His brown leather jacket could transition from snow in Aspen to the warmer weather in Denver, and his lightweight hiking boots worked for either climate. After he slid his second Glock into a shoulder holster, he went downstairs to get his laptop.

Before they joined his friend at the Roaring Fork private airfield, they needed to make a stop at Uncle Walter's place, where Shane had already arranged to drop off Elvis. He couldn't very well drag the dog into town. Though his black Lab had a harness proclaiming his training as a therapy dog, a lot of places didn't make exceptions for any canines. Besides, the only other time he'd taken Elvis on the chopper, the dog had been "all shook up" for a week.

It felt like he'd covered all the bases. Since he'd kept Mallory safe overnight, he figured he was doing a decent job as a bodyguard. His phone calls and PI investigating had made progress toward finding her mom. Best of all, he and Mallory had gone deeper in their connection. *To the deepest level, the mermaid level.* He imagined her long silky hair streaming behind them as they joined together in a warm soothing sea. No more need to wonder if there was a future for them.

At the foot of the staircase, Elvis dashed toward him, nervously woofing and panting and spinning in a circle.

"What's wrong, dude?"

Then he heard Mallory shout, "How did you get my phone number?"

Shane charged past the dog and went into her bedroom. She'd promised to hand over her phone after one more call to Sylvia—a promise that came too late. She held up her phone and hit the speaker button so he could hear both sides of the conversation.

"How, indeed. You gave me your card and your personal number when I visited Reflections." The speaker had a baritone voice with an unusual accent, a combination of British and Middle Eastern. "You sound upset. Why is that?"

"You've had dealings with my family in the past. You should have told me." She looked at Shane and whispered, "It's Conrad Burdock."

"I fear you have drawn some unfortunate conclusions, young lady. I mean you no harm. In fact, I have a proposition for you."

"Why would I ever hook up with you? Your thugs charged into my gallery with guns blazing. They chased us through the streets in a Hummer and put bullet holes in my friend's car."

"Do not be absurd. It was never my intention to injure you or frighten you. The opposite is true. I hope to catch more flies with honey."

"What are you talking about?"

"Listen to me, Mallory. I believe, sincerely believe, we can work together. You and I can find the African Teardrop and return the gem to the people of Sierra Leone."

Shane noticed a softening at the edges of Mallory's turquoise eyes, and he could tell that the idea of returning the stone to its rightful owners appealed to her. In spite of Burdock's melodious voice, he recognized the words of a con man who'd say anything to get what he wanted.

"Why should I trust you?" Mallory asked.

"I have lived in Africa for most of my life. I love the land and the wildlife. I understand the people, their customs and their ways. With proceeds from the sale of the Teardrop, we could fight the extreme poverty afflicting Sierra Leone. We could provide wholesome food and medicine for the children. We could build schools."

Shane gripped her free hand and whispered, "Don't fall for his pitch."

But her tender heart had been touched. "Suppose I agree to go along with you, what do you want me to do?"

"We must get your sister out of the way. I am sorry to inform you, but Amber DeSilva is a liar and a cheat. If you and I talk to your mother, she will see things my way. She will want to do the right thing."

"Give me a minute." She muted the phone and made eye contact with Shane. "I believe what he's saying. Mom would want to help the starving children."

"Hey, I'm the last person to say your sister is trustworthy, but I believe her more than this crook. Don't forget the guys in ski masks with guns."

"Right." She unmuted the phone. "You said the men who attacked us at Reflections weren't connected with you."

"Correct."

"If they aren't working for you, who sent them?"

"Once again, I must be the bearer of sad tidings. Forgive me." He cleared his throat. "I have every reason to believe that the culprit is none other than Raymond DeSilva. Your papa."

"But he's dead."

"And so is your mother, Ingrid Stromberg DeSilva." A low chuckle. "Yet, she appears to be extremely active."

Was he suggesting that both Mallory's mother and father faked their deaths? Not a chance! The odds against two faked deaths in one family were astronomical. Shane vigorously shook his head and gestured for her to mute the call again.

"Please excuse me," she said.

"I am out of time. Must dash. Think of all I have said."

"Wait!" Mallory's voice rang with urgency. "Amber said you killed my father."

"Consider the source," he said darkly. "Farewell, Mallory. I shall be in touch."

The call ended. She sank onto the unmade bed and waved the blank screen of the phone in Shane's direction. "This is a perfect illustration of why I need to keep my phone with me."

"So you can get calls from murderous international liars?"

He took the phone away from her and pulled out the battery, hoping he had disabled Burdock's ability to trace their location. They needed to get rid of the phone as soon as possible.

"What if he's telling the truth?" She'd already dressed in jeans and a forest green sweater. Sitting on the edge of the bed, she stuck her feet into her hiking boots. "I like the idea of giving the Teardrop back to Sierra Leone."

"Let me look into the background for Raymond DeSilva.

When Amber told us he was dead, I crossed him off my list of suspects."

She flopped back on the bed. "When I was just a kid, I used to dream about having a real father. A handsome prince or a dashing explorer like Indiana Jones or a rock star. In the screen photo Amber showed me, he's almost handsome with his black hair and mustache. Maybe I can still meet him."

And maybe that wasn't such a good idea. If her father was still alive, he had a stronger motive than anyone else to come after her mom and reclaim the Teardrop. Twenty-six years ago, Gloria had faked her death and stolen a fortune in precious gems from him.

Shane knelt before her and finished tying her bootlaces. When he stood, he pulled her into his arms. Keeping Mallory safe was becoming more complicated by the minute.

AT THE ROARING FORK private airfield outside Aspen, the runways and tarmac surrounding several hangars were cleared of snow. Sunlight glistened on the white wings of the small aircraft and the blades of helos. Mallory and Shane had been rushing since they left his house. She looked down at his laptop, which she held on her lap. The minute when Burdock had claimed her father was still alive, she'd wanted to do a computer search for Raymond DeSilva. As soon as she got a chance…

First, they'd dropped off Elvis. Not an easy task. Though the dog had politely accepted treats from Uncle Walter and allowed himself to be petted, he kept firing sad pathetic looks in their direction. She'd assured him that they'd be back. If he was a good boy, he'd have a lovely time with sweet, kindly Uncle Walter. Then Shane had taken her phone away and given it to Walter for safekeeping. She felt naked without it.

When they'd returned to the Navigator, she'd used Shane's phone to make a few calls and ascertained that Steve Fordham, the pilot who might have given Mom a ride to Brooklyn kept his fleet at the Roaring Fork facility. He wasn't in his office, but she hoped she could talk to someone who worked for him.

They were making progress. Slowly.

Shane parked the Navigator outside an arched metal hangar that was the size of a small warehouse. Under the curved roof, she could see two helicopters with green bodies and striped yellow and black blades. Though she'd gone on helo rides before, Mallory wasn't really comfortable with flying. Not that there was anything to fear with Shane at her side.

She looked toward him, appreciating his confident grin and steady gaze. Once again, he held his phone toward her. "Give Amber a call. Find out where she's staying and if she's uncovered any new information."

"I don't want to talk to her."

His smile didn't falter. "Don't tell me you trust that Burdock weasel more than your long-lost sister."

"Okay, I won't tell you." She snatched the phone from him. "After this, I want to run over to Fordham's hangar and see if somebody can verify his trip to New York with Mom."

"I can do that while you talk to Amber."

She patted his cheek, not intending to notice how fine-looking he was in the clear, sunny morning light. But she couldn't help herself. A warm sexy feeling started in her belly and spread through her body. "Fordham's office staff will be more willing to talk to me because I'm Gloria's daughter."

"And I'm an Olympic skier." He stroked her hair, tucking a strand back into the messy bun on the top of her head. "In most places, nobody cares about my rep, but here in Aspen I'm kind of a superstar."

"You might want to check that ego before you talk to anybody."

"I think Fordham's people will understand." He gestured to three nearby hangars with the name Fordham written in oversize wildly egotistical letters. He opened the car door and stepped out. "Wish me luck."

"Don't break a leg."

Watching him jog toward the Fordham hangars, Mallory decided that Shane had made a full recovery from his injuries. No limp. No hitch in his step. He seemed to be a man at the peak of his physical powers, but she knew that wasn't true. Before his accident, he'd been an elite world-class athlete. Being merely "above average" had to be disappointing. Last night, she'd been blown away by the perfect proportions of his naked body. Never would she forget the way he strutted across the bedroom like the king of the castle. But she'd noticed the scars from operations on his legs. Were they imperfections or badges of courage that came from overcoming adversity?

She hoped to have a long time to figure Shane out, but now she had more pressing issues. She flipped open the laptop. Though it would probably be best to wait until she had some quiet time to explore on the internet, she just couldn't wait any longer. She typed in the codes he'd shown her to bypass his cyber security and access the Internet. The browser lit up. Entering her father's name brought up several possibilities. While she sorted through them, she called her sister, hoping to be able to leave a message. Unfortunately, Amber picked up after the fourth ring.

"It's me," Mallory said. "Did you find a place to stay?"

"Brown Palace Hotel in downtown Denver. It's old-fashioned, surprisingly charming."

"Why surprising?"

"Well, it's Denver, after all. Not a place I associate with class."

"You're showing your ignorance." Mallory hated the way some people put down the city. Denver hadn't been a backwoods cow town for decades. "Denver is very sophisticated."

"Whatever."

She sounded like a spoiled eye-rolling teenager. Amber epitomized many attitudes Mallory disliked, and she'd already decided not to tell her sister about Burdock. There was no problem sharing her conversation with Mom. "She called earlier this morning."

"Ingrid?"

Mallory didn't bother correcting her. "It seems that Mom stayed with a Denver artist. Her name is Hannah Wye."

Amber verified the spelling and promised to look her up. "What else?"

"She mentioned her good friend Felix." Only half concentrating on her talk with Amber, she sorted through computer entries until she found a likely thread to follow. "Have you contacted him?"

"Matter of fact, I have." There was a hesitation in Amber's voice. Was she lying? "Felix and I made an appointment for a one o'clock lunch at the Ship Tavern at the hotel. Too bad you won't be able to get to Denver in time for that meeting."

Mallory smiled to herself. *Oh, yes, I will.* "What about the guy from the museum? Ty Rivera. Have you spoken to him?"

"I left a message. I'll check back later. When do you expect to get here?"

"We haven't left Aspen yet," Mallory said truthfully. The laptop screen filled with a photograph of Raymond DeSilva—a dashing gent with distinguished silver streaks at his temples. "I'll call when we're near the Brown. I have a good feeling about our investigation. We might find her today."

"Forget her," Amber said. "We might find the diamond."

At least her sister was consistent. Her priority had always been to find the Teardrop, and she'd never pretended to care about their mother. For her, the investigation was all about the money.

When she ended the call, Mallory concentrated fully on her internet search and read her father's biography. Raymond DeSilva was very much alive, living in Johannesburg. Why had her sister lied to her? Amber had to know about Raymond DeSilva. He didn't seem to be making any attempt to hide. Photos of his estate showed a gleaming modern mansion constructed of geometric shapes, similar to the facets on a diamond. His trophy wife couldn't have been much older than Mallory.

She had a father. Should have been good news. She should have been excited, happy, fascinated. Truthfully, she just didn't care.

Chapter Fourteen

Shane couldn't say she hadn't warned him. Mallory had told him about her phobia regarding air travel. During the hour and a half helicopter flight from the airfield outside Aspen to a small airport south of Denver, she'd gone from clutching his hand in a finger-crushing grip to a somewhat more relaxed state of panic. Two or three times, she'd peered through the plexiglass bubble of the helo at the earth below. Together, they'd watched the snow-topped mountains recede into valleys and rocky foothills, which morphed into houses and streets and highways packed with vehicles. Her momentary fascination faded quickly, and her eyelids squeezed shut. Not sleeping but denying the queasy fear that churned in her gut.

Her phobia might have been worsened by the unsettling discovery that Amber had lied and Mallory's father—the father she'd never met—was alive. When Shane saw the computer article about Raymond DeSilva, he kicked himself for not taking the time to research the guy when his name first came up. But it didn't make sense for Amber to pretend she didn't know he was alive. Why tell them a fairy tale that could be so easily disproved?

He wondered if Amber arrogantly assumed he and Mallory were idiots and would never figure it out. Or she might be keeping Raymond DeSilva out of the picture to protect him from his enemies like Burdock. Speaking of that devil, Burdock had offered a reasonable explanation for Amber's deception: she and her father were working together to get the Teardrop. By claiming he was dead, she'd hoped to divert suspicion from them both.

When they climbed out of the helo and stepped onto the airport's tarmac, Mallory flung herself into his arms and squeezed with all her strength. "Sorry to be such a baby."

"You did fine." He held her close, pleased by the way they fit together. He enjoyed being her rock—the guy who protected her, even though she was far from helpless. "All the same, I wouldn't mind driving back to Aspen when we're done here. Instead of flying."

"I'd like that." She pivoted, gave their pilot a less emphatic embrace and thanked him for the ride.

"No prob." He shrugged his narrow shoulders and adjusted his aviator shades to deal with the brilliant Denver sunlight. "I've got a couple of things I need to do in the city, and I already lined up a vehicle. You guys need a ride into town?"

"I've got it covered." Shane had ordered a rental car to be delivered to the small terminal with attached offices, a lounge and coffee shop. "There's somebody I need to talk to before we head out."

While Mallory and the pilot walked to the terminal, Shane made his way to Hangar D where Steve Fordham rented space for his planes when he was in Denver. His assistant in Aspen had told Shane that Fordham would be at this airport from ten o'clock until noon, and he wanted to meet this guy in person. It seemed obvious that Fordham had given Gloria a ride to New York, but Shane sensed there was more to the story.

In the small lounge attached to the hangar, he found the CEO of Fordham Aviation sprawled on an uncomfortable-looking love seat with metal arms. His long legs stretched out in front of him, and a blue baseball cap with his logo—a huge *F* and smaller *ordham*—shaded his eyes.

Shane sat in the chair opposite. "Steve Fordham," he said.

"Who wants to know?"

"Shane Reilly. I'm a PI working for Mallory Greenfield."

"And you want to know if I gave Gloria a ride to New York." Fordham sat up straight, took off his cap and stared at Shane with intense blue eyes that contrasted his dark leathery tan. "I took her there. She called me about a week ago and asked if I could give her a lift. It's a trip we've made a couple of times before, and I don't mind helping her out."

The aviator didn't seem like the sort of guy who did favors out of the goodness of his heart. "Are you and Gloria dating?"

"I wish." He flashed an over-whitened smile and licked his lips suggestively. "She's a fine-looking woman. A little old for my taste but still hot. Like her daughter. Am I right?"

Shane wasn't amused by the creepy playboy attitude. "You must have heard about the search for Gloria in Aspen. It's big news."

"Yeah, I guess. Everybody thinks Aspen is so sophisticated, but it's really just a small town where everybody gets up into everybody else's business. Some of my passengers are movie stars and royalty, but they're no different than you or me. Do you remember that Swedish super-model who plays a space cop? Bang, bang, bang, she's a real tasty meatball. And then—"

Before he could list all the famous people who had flown with Fordham Aviation, Shane got back on topic. "Why didn't you notify the police? Let them know Gloria was okay."

"She asked me not to tell anybody."

"You don't seem like the kind of guy who lets somebody else call the shots." Shane took a jab at Fordham's ego. "I'm guessing Gloria has some kind of leverage over you."

His gaze slid sideways, evading direct eye contact. "She's my agent."

Shane had all but forgotten the artist-to-agent part of their relationship. "Gloria must have a lot of contacts in New York."

"You bet she does." He stood and stabbed at Shane with his index finger. "The woman represents Walter Pulaski, and he makes big bucks. If she could get a couple of my paintings into galleries in Manhattan, my work might catch on. I'm a pilot who paints the sky. That's a good hook, right?"

"Not exactly unexpected."

"As if you're an expert." He took two angry strides toward the exit. "Besides, I figured the guy who drove her to the airfield would be responsible and talk to the sheriff."

Finally, he'd said something interesting. Shane jumped to his feet. "What guy?"

"You know who." He reached for the doorknob.

Much as he hated chasing Fordham, Shane dodged around the chair and blocked the exit. Gloria's disappearance might be a joke to this flyboy who was a legend in his own mind, but Mallory was nearly devastated. And there was a twenty-million-dollar diamond involved. He pinned Fordham with a gaze. "I want a name."

"Okey dokey." He scoffed, mocking the lighthearted word. "That's how he talks. Howdy-doody and diddly-do and great googly-moogly."

"A name."

"The vice president at Fidelity Union, Drew Sherman."

Everybody in town knew Sherman. The husky man with heavy black eyebrows had a smile for every patron of the bank and an encyclopedic memory for jokes. He played Santa at the Christmas Carnival and was known as a family man. "What was he doing with Gloria?"

"Not sure," Fordham admitted. "He didn't come into the hangar to say hello, but I saw him arguing with her outside his car. When she came inside, I asked about Sherman, and she told me that they'd been associates for years."

His inflection when he said *associates* made Shane wonder if there was more to the story. It seemed like Gloria had a lot of male friends, ranging from Uncle Walter to Fordham to Felix to the local banker. "Do you know anything else about their relationship?"

"I'd say they were palsy-walsy." He smirked at the corn-ball phrase, which he obviously intended to make fun of Sherman. "She's known him for years, ever since Mallory dated his son in high school. Get your mind out of the gutter, Shane."

"Occupational hazard." Private investigators tended to see the worst in everybody, and they were often correct when it came to cheating spouses and lying businessmen. Shane missed the more straightforward world occupied by his police officer brother and father.

"Anything else?" Fordham asked.

Shane figured he might as well tie up loose ends. "You flew Gloria back to Denver from New York."

"That's right."

"Will you be taking her back to Aspen?"

"She's not on my schedule. I dropped her off a couple of days ago and haven't seen her since. I suppose if her timing worked out, I'd give her a lift. No point in alienating an agent, right?"

His body language didn't indicate deception, but Fordham had folded his arms across his chest, which usually meant a closed-down or unfriendly attitude. No surprise. The pilot walked a shaky tightrope between civil and hostile. He never actually said anything offensive but implied a lot.

Figuring he had nothing to lose, Shane introduced the multimillion-dollar question. "Did Gloria mention a special object that she was taking to New York?"

"Like what?"

His gaze turned shifty. Shane wondered how involved Fordham was in Gloria's disappearance. Was he more than a hapless dupe who wanted to get on his agent's good side? "Forget I said anything."

"Come on, man. You can tell me. Are you talking about some kind of artwork?"

"You might call it that." Again, Shane studied the other man's body language, looking for clues. "When I think about this object, I want to cry. To shed a teardrop."

Fordham looked confused. Apparently, the word *teardrop* meant nothing to him. "Have it your way. I don't care what kind of game she's playing. Are we done here?"

"Afraid so."

After this little talk with Fordham, Shane didn't feel much closer to finding the elusive Gloria Greenfield or the diamond she'd stolen twenty-six years ago. He'd ask Mallory about Drew Sherman but doubted there was anything more than a friend giving another friend a lift to the airport. Maybe they'd have better luck with Amber.

AT TEN MINUTES past one o'clock, she and Shane dropped off their rental car at the valet station and strolled into the Brown Palace Hotel in downtown Denver. As she crossed the luxurious lobby, Mallory flashed back to her junior year in high school when she attended the Rocky Mountain Debutante Ball at the Brown. The event was an unaccustomed splash of glamour in her super-casual lifestyle. For her, getting dressed up meant wearing clean jeans, which was what she had on right now—black jeans, hiking boots and a cashmere sweater set in deep burgundy. Her simple pearl necklace was a gift from a boyfriend and couldn't have possibly come from the stash Mom had supposedly stolen.

"The first time I came into this hotel," she said as she fingered the pearls, "I was wearing a coral chiffon gown. Long and ruffled in the back. Short in the front. With a halter neck because I didn't have the boobs to hold up a strapless. Still don't."

"There's nothing wrong with your boobs," Shane said. "Was it a debutante ball?"

"How'd you guess?"

"I got roped into escorting girlfriends to a couple of those things. Always wore the same black suit."

"Men have it easy when it comes to fancy events. My date for that dance was Josh Sherman, the football star."

Her family had known his for nearly ten years, and it came as no surprise when Shane told her that Mr. Sherman gave Mom a ride to the airfield. But why hadn't he mentioned it to her when she stopped by the bank? Or to the sheriff when he was involved in the search? Mr. Sherman wasn't the sort of person who kept secrets unless he had a very good reason. The obvious inference was an affair, but she couldn't imagine the straight-arrow banker cheating on his wife of thirty years.

She straightened her shoulders when they paused at the hostess desk in the Ship Tavern. Like the prow of a galleon, the restaurant was located at the front of the triangle-shaped red sandstone hotel. The decor and the long bar suggested a vintage pub with polished wood and leather booths. The ship fixtures—such an odd metaphor for Denver—included a thick mast and crow's nest with an old-fashioned ship's clock. She spotted Amber and Felix at a table halfway across the floor. Her sister was blithely sipping a margarita.

Amber's carefree attitude lit the fuse on Mallory's anger. She felt a red flush rising on her cheeks, and she clutched Shane's hand, needing his self-control before she confronted her sister, who had lied about the death of their father and had done nothing to help in the search for Gloria.

"Hey." Shane summoned her attention. "Don't explode until after we find out what she knows."

"Don't worry. I can control myself."

He looked doubtful. "Maybe I should do the talking."

"I've got this." She set her mouth in a rigid smile as she approached Felix Komenda, who rose politely from his chair to shake her hand. "We met at Reflections in Aspen. I'm Mallory."

"Of course." He was as tall as Shane—slender, poised and graceful. Under his blazer, Mallory knew he had full-sleeve tattoos. "Even if I did not remember our first meeting, I would know you ladies are sisters."

True, they resembled each other. Today, they both happened to be wearing similar shades of mauve. Mallory had pulled her long hair up into a knot on top of her head. Amber's neatly styled hair was a nearly identical blond. The sisters glared at each other with matching turquoise eyes.

Amber stated the obvious. "You're here."

"Surprised?"

"I thought it would take longer to drive."

"Which is why we decided to fly," Mallory said. "Shane's friend runs a helicopter service."

The two men shook hands like civilized human beings while the sisters faced off like a couple of lionesses sizing each other up before going in for the kill. Mallory had never been this furious. Her sister had done more than subtly betray her trust. Amber had outright lied.

"I am so very pleased to see you," Felix said in an accented melodic voice. "Please sit down. Would you care for a drink?"

When Shane pulled out her chair and guided her into it, she was grateful for his assistance. Her legs and arms were tense and stiff, nearly immoveable. "I'll stick to water."

"An upset stomach, perhaps?" Felix regarded her with what appeared to be genuine sympathy. "Your mother mentioned that you are an anxious flyer."

Not allowing herself to be distracted from her outrage, Mallory's glare at her sister intensified. "I'm fine."

Under the table, Shane took her hand, holding her back from the hostility that simmered so near the surface. "We have a few questions."

"Right," Mallory snapped, ready to get down to business. They had an investigation to pursue, and she didn't intend to waste time. "Mr. Komenda, have you spoken to my mother recently?"

His gleaming smile highlighted his mocha brown skin. The last time Mallory had seen him, his head was shaved. Now his hair was closely trimmed, and he wasn't bald. His onyx eyes held a depth of unreadable expression. "Gloria and I met for brunch."

"Her name is Ingrid," Amber said. "I don't know why you people insist on using her alias. She is now and has always been Ingrid DeSilva."

"For purposes of clarity," Felix said, "I will refer to her as Gloria, the name she chose for herself rather than the one she was given. I believe it is a woman's right to name herself."

"Absolutely," Mallory said. "I like the way you think."

"You would." Amber turned to Felix and stuck her tongue out at him like an angry kindergartner. "You're never on my side."

"My dear child, I have watched over you from when you were an energetic four-year-old. I documented your life in hundreds of letters to Gloria and—"

"Ingrid," she interrupted.

When he stretched his long arm and touched her hand, his collar—which was open four buttons—spread wider, and Mallory caught a glimpse of the topmost branches of the Cotton Tree in Freetown tattooed on his chest. When he spoke to Amber, he was gentle. "You must trust me, child. I will always do what is best for you."

"Then tell me…" In contrast, her voice was harsh. "Where is the African Teardrop?"

"I do not know."

"Don't know?" She flung his hand away from her. "Or won't say?"

"I speak the truth."

"You've always been on Ingrid's side. Never on mine," she snarled. "You've been lying to me since I was a little girl."

Mallory surged to her feet. "You're a fine one to talk about lies. You claimed my father was dead. Not so. Raymond DeSilva is living with his new wife in South Africa."

"She's a bitch. And so are you." On the opposite side of the small table, Amber stood to confront her. "I never should have contacted you. You and your broken-down-skier-turned-investigator have been useless. He and his ugly mutt are a joke."

"I can believe that you think I'm a bitch. Making an allowance for rudeness, I can accept your snide comment about Shane. But nobody, and I mean absolutely nobody, insults Elvis." Mallory snatched the water glass from beside Felix's place setting and flung the contents into her sister's face.

Gasping, Amber stared as water dripped down her chin onto her silk blouse. She huffed and puffed, unable to speak. Nose in the air, she stalked away from the table.

Mallory had no regret for what she'd done. In fact, she wished she'd ordered a cocktail to throw. Something big and messy like a Bloody Mary.

Chapter Fifteen

When Felix took a step toward the exit from the Ship Tavern to follow Amber, Shane gestured for him to return to the table. "Stay with us."

"I must be certain that she is all right."

"She'll recover. It was only water."

Much as Shane might have hoped that Amber had been drenched in goop or splashed with permanent dye, Mallory's attack had been benign—wild and a little bit shocking but still harmless. It was time for him—the so-called broken-down skier/investigator—to take charge and start tying up loose ends. He waited for Felix to sit, then signaled the waiter who had been hovering nearby, waiting for their drama to fizzle. "I'll have a Guinness on tap."

The waiter nodded to Mallory. "And for the lady?"

"A Bloody Mary."

"Very well." The waiter glanced at the vacant chair. "Will she be returning?"

"Don't know," Shane said. After the waiter left, he leaned across the table toward Felix. "We have questions that will be easier for you to answer without Amber hanging over your shoulder."

Felix nodded. "Perhaps."

"From what I understand, you've been watching over

her since she was four and her mother faked her own death."

Felix affirmed the somewhat outrageous statement, and Shane had to wonder why this seemingly sane, sophisticated man would accept Gloria's criminal intentions. Why would he agree to watch over a child he barely knew? There must be some way he benefited from this relationship. "Why?"

"Of course, I cared about the child. Amber can be endearing. However, she has not outgrown a habit of throwing tantrums and making ridiculous demands."

A lovable child abandoned and needing help was a partial explanation, but Shane sensed a more compelling, more personal reason. He couldn't believe that Felix—a man of the world—would dedicate his life to Amber because he liked the kid. Maybe he was looking for a way to escape Sierra Leone. "You stayed with her family in New York. Was it difficult to get a green card?"

"I have United States citizenship. I was born in Atlanta, Georgia. My parents moved to Sierra Leone when I was a toddler. I consider both countries to be my home."

Immigration hadn't been an issue, but there were other advantages to living in America. "When you came here, did you go to college?"

"Oh, yes, I attended several art schools and academies in New York. Also, I worked in galleries, like Reflections." He beamed at Mallory. "I was pleased when Gloria told me what she was doing in Aspen."

Everything he said made sense, but Shane wasn't close to satisfied. The story lacked important connections. "Tell me about Amber's father. Are you close to him?"

He exhaled a weary sigh and shook his head. "Raymond DeSilva paid me to act as Amber's nanny and body-guard—"

"Excuse me," Mallory interrupted. "Why does she need a bodyguard?"

"Much as I hate to bear more bad news, your father has enemies, legions of enemies. Need I remind you of Conrad Burdock?"

"I guess not," she said.

"I worked for DeSilva, but we were never friends. His lying, cheating, thievery and violence disgusted me. I hated him for the way he abused Gloria."

"Physically?" Mallory asked in a voice shaking with anger or grief or both. "Did he physically hurt her?"

"Yes," Felix said. "Gloria tried to make her marriage work, but she could not change her husband. Leaving him was the best decision she ever made. She is a strong, wise woman."

Shane heard the anger in his voice when he talked about DeSilva, which was counterbalanced by affection when he mentioned Gloria's name, and that explained a lot. The puzzle pieces were falling into place. Felix had taken care of little Amber because he had deep, intimate feelings for her mother, maybe even loved her.

A familiar pattern began to form. Shane couldn't explain, but he recognized intuitively what was happening. *Gloria Greenfield is magic.* As she floated through life being irresponsible and creative, she cast magical spells that drew people, mostly men, to do her bidding. Walter Pulaski called her his muse. Fordham, the misogynist pilot, rearranged his schedule to fly her to New York, free of charge. And Felix Komenda had devoted over a decade of his life to babysitting her daughter.

When the waiter returned with their drinks, he glanced

over at Mallory as she tucked a long strand of gleaming blond hair behind her ear. The crimson flush of anger that colored her cheeks had faded to a pinkish hue, and her mouth curved in a smile. *She's magical, too.* He'd do anything for another taste of those soft full lips.

They tipped their glasses toward each other and sipped. In unison, they turned toward Felix. Shane hated to leave the relationship part of this complicated story behind, but they might not have much time before Amber came charging back into the Tavern. "I have to ask about the Teardrop."

Felix laced his long slender fingers together and rested his hands on the tabletop. "This story covers many, many years. I shall try to condense my narrative. At 521 carats, the African Teardrop ranks among the finest stones found in Sierra Leone. The pale blue gem—with the color and glitter of a perfect teardrop—is worth more than twenty million and symbolizes the dichotomy between the natural wealth of the nation and the poverty of the people who live there. Shortly after the Teardrop was discovered in 1968 and displayed to the world, it disappeared. Everyone assumed it was stolen and sold as a blood diamond or hidden in the private vault of a wealthy collector."

Shane knew a little bit about the tragedy of blood diamonds, also called conflict diamonds. During his prime, he'd skied off-piste in the Atlas Mountains of northern Africa and had been approached by warlords and terrorists who offered to sell him gems at cut-rate prices—a heinous, tragic bargain. The real cost came in the suffering of the people who were forced to give up these treasures and barely had enough to feed their families. The United Nations and the Kimberley Process system were involved in regulating the sales of gems and marketing them as "conflict-free."

This history didn't explain what had happened to the Teardrop. "How did the gem fall into the hands of Raymond DeSilva?"

"We will never know," Felix said. "When Gloria scooped up Raymond's inventory before his shop in Freetown was bombed and burned to the ground, she did not know the Teardrop was among the other stones. After she left Sierra Leone, she discovered the treasure. And this is where I come into the story."

"You had an interest in the gem," Shane said.

"Of course." He winced at a distant but still remembered heartache. "The African Teardrop is a national treasure in addition to the monetary value. Gloria was aware of this heritage. She wished to return the gem, making sure that it went to the right people. I offered my help, and she accepted."

"A hell of a huge responsibility."

"Yes."

"How old were you at the time?"

"Twenty-six." He nodded to Mallory. "The same age as you."

"And my mom when she left Africa," she said. "I hope I can step up the way you both did and make things right. The Teardrop could provide funding for hospitals and schools, alleviating suffering and truly helping the people of Sierra Leone."

"The opposite is equally true," Felix warned. "For decades, conflict diamonds have financed warlords and terrorists. The Teardrop might be used to pay for a slaughter. This is a most delicate political situation."

Shane wanted to get back to his narrative. "When you realized that Gloria had the Teardrop, what did you do?"

"I was young and needed guidance. My parents had many contacts, but they were spending more time in the United States because of the civil war in Sierra Leone. Government officials were corrupt. Some of the rebels were admirable. Others were pure evil. No one seemed worthy. None could help me. I didn't know who I could trust."

"I understand," Mallory said. "Not knowing who to believe can paralyze you."

"When it came to the Teardrop, you and Gloria were faced with difficult decisions," Shane said. "You didn't want to make a mistake."

Felix paused to take a sip of his beer. "And so, we did nothing."

"You told no one about the Teardrop?"

"Gloria's escape from DeSilva seemed to be successful. No one knew where she had gone. They weren't following her. They believed her to be dead."

A miracle. Again, Shane thought of Gloria's secret weapon—a magic that caused criminals to provide her with perfectly forged identification and gemologists, like Ty Rivera at the Museum of Nature and Science, who helped her sell the precious stones. Uncle Walter got her settled in Aspen, which couldn't have been an easy proposition. And she'd made a living for herself and her infant daughter with an art gallery. Not the most lucrative or stable occupation.

Felix continued, "She hid the Teardrop. For twenty-six years, we kept the secret."

With rapt attention, Mallory asked, "What changed?"

"DeSilva."

"Did he find her?"

"To be honest, I do not know." Felix lifted his beer mug to his lips and took another taste. "She started receiving odd emails and texts. On the street outside Hotel Jerome, she thought she saw him. More than once, she heard his voice, threatening her. And she found objects in her house missing or misplaced, including mementos that DeSilva would know were important to her. Frightened, she believed she must return the Teardrop before DeSilva got his hands on it."

The new revelation opened other doors for investigation, namely he needed to track the location of Raymond DeSilva. Shane had several questions, but he caught sight of Amber at the entrance to Ship Tavern, and knew they were about to be interrupted. He asked Felix, "Who is Hannah Wye and how does she fit in?"

"She's a watercolor artist."

"And also an attorney," Felix added. "Her services might be needed while dealing with the return of the Teardrop. And she offered Gloria use of her downtown loft last night."

Shane pressed forward. "Why did Gloria go to the fence in Brooklyn?"

"A mistake." Felix shook his head. "I suspect she planned to easily sell the gem and be done with it. Instead, her actions alerted Amber and Conrad Burdock."

"What can you tell me about Ty Rivera at the museum? Can he be trusted?"

"I hope so. Gloria went to see him at lunchtime. I wanted to accompany her, but she insisted on talking to Rivera alone."

"Mallory has an appointment with him," Shane said. "In less than two hours."

"Rivera has excellent contacts in Sierra Leone. His advice would be highly beneficial."

Keeping his voice low, Shane asked, "How can I reach Gloria?"

"I fear you must wait for her to contact you."

"Is she returning to Aspen?"

"I do not know."

"Stay in touch, Felix. I'll do the same."

Amber stormed around the table and returned to her seat. With a nasty smirk, she stared at Mallory and lifted her stemmed margarita glass. The tip of her tongue licked salt from the rim. Mallory did the same with her Bloody Mary, which was a much more destructive drink than the water she'd flung before. It seemed apparent that neither of these women was inclined to apologize for the prior argument. He would have liked to probe into Amber's relationship with her father but doubted she'd tell him the truth. When the people in this dysfunctional family took sides, she was firmly on Team DeSilva.

He pushed back his chair and stood. "We should be going."

"Oh, I don't think so," Amber said. "You won't get away from me that easily. I want to know what you've found out about the Teardrop. I've waited a lifetime for that inheritance, and I deserve every penny."

Mallory stood tall and straightened her shoulders. "You and your father stay away from me and Gloria. We owe you nothing."

Shane tossed a couple of twenties on the table and took Mallory's hand. Together, they left the Ship Tavern and went to the valet station on the street. He glanced over his shoulder at the charming old hotel. "Should I make a reservation? We could stay here tonight."

"With Amber down the hall?" She shook her head, and another strand of hair slipped out of her loosely knotted bun. "This hotel isn't big enough for the both of us."

"Still, I hate to pass up a night without Elvis. Just you and me."

"I miss the dog."

When their rental car pulled up to the valet station, he held the door open for her. "We're early for our appointment with Rivera, but I wouldn't mind taking a walk around Ferril Lake at City Park."

"Perfect." She turned her face up to the sun, unfastened her bun and let her silky golden hair cascade down her back. "When we get back to Aspen, we're looking at snow and cold. While we're here, it's nice to enjoy the autumn."

He slipped behind the steering wheel and drove east on Seventeenth Avenue. Brilliant sunshine glistened on the red maples and golden aspens that still had their leaves. He'd grown up in Denver and loved the temperate October weather, perfect for jogging, biking and football.

After he parked near the lake, he noticed a commotion in the parking lot outside the Museum of Nature and Science that overlooked a fountain and rose garden. Though there was no sound from sirens, red and blue police lights flashed against the granite walls of the four-story rectangular building that housed dinosaur skeletons, dioramas of hundreds of animals and impressive rocks and mineral displays.

"I have a bad feeling about those police lights," he said.

"Me, too."

His cell phone jangled. A call from Logan.

His brother got right to the point. "Last night, you asked me to research credit cards for Ingrid DeSilva, Ingrid Stromberg and Gloria Greenfield."

"And I appreciate your help." Already he didn't like the direction of this conversation.

"Did you find the woman?"

"I haven't laid eyes on her," Shane said truthfully. "What's the problem?"

"This woman—let's call her Gloria—had a lunch meeting at the Museum of Nature and Science with the gemologist in charge of the precious stones exhibits. She was last seen in his company at the café in the museum. His name is Ty Rivera. Do you know him?"

Once again, Shane could be completely honest without implicating Mallory or her mom. "Never met the guy."

"I have another name for you," Logan said. His voice sharpened, and Shane recognized the tone from when they were kids and Logan was about to give him a hard time. "Mallory Greenfield."

No way to sidestep that one. "I know her. Why do you ask?"

"I made some phone calls to the cops in Aspen and found out that Mallory is the daughter of Gloria, the woman you asked me to trace. She's been missing for seven days."

"Right."

"I was thinking that maybe, just maybe, Mallory hired you to find her mother. Is she your client?"

As a cop, his brother ought to recognize the confidentiality issues involved in being a private investigator. "Can't tell you," Shane said.

Life would have been easier if he could have honestly

talked to Logan, confided everything they'd learned about Gloria and the African Teardrop. He wanted his brother's help in tracking down Gloria and DeSilva and Conrad Burdock. But he couldn't betray Mallory. He refused to be the person responsible for sending her mom to jail.

"Your friend Mallory also has an appointment scheduled with Ty Rivera. At half past three." Logan paused, waiting for him to fill the silence. When Shane didn't speak, his brother continued, "If you have contact with her, you can tell Mallory Greenfield that Mr. Rivera won't be able to meet with her."

Dreading the answer, Shane asked, "Why is that?"

"Your client is knee-deep in a stinking pile of trouble, buddy. I know you're trying to protect her. I get it. But you're both going to get hurt. You've got to tell me whatever you know."

"Why can't she meet with Rivera?"

"He's dead. Murdered. His throat slashed by an ancient Mesoamerican obsidian blade from one of the museum exhibits."

Chapter Sixteen

A loud disorderly gaggle of Canadian geese waddled along the paved path encircling Ferril Lake at City Park. Mallory tried to disregard their raucous honking and eavesdrop on Shane's phone call. His part in the conversation sounded noncommittal, but still she worried. His brother was a cop, an occupation which represented a heavy-duty threat to Mom. Never mind that her crimes didn't hurt anyone except her abusive husband. For twenty-six years, she'd paid her taxes and been a model citizen notwithstanding her eccentricity. None of that mattered. Because she'd faked her death and assumed a false identity, she was considered a criminal, and it was Logan's job to arrest her.

When Shane ended his call, he stood for a moment, staring at the screen on his cell phone, giving her a chance to appreciate his tousled sun-streaked hair and tanned complexion. His ridiculously long eyelashes drew her attention to his caramel-colored eyes. The way he'd looked at her last night set off a chain reaction unlike anything she'd felt before. If he wanted to turn Mom over to the police, Mallory didn't think she could bear it.

He tried to smile, but his mouth was tense. "I just got a text from Pulaski. Gloria called your phone, and he's passing on the message."

Her heart skipped a beat. "Is she all right?"

"Yes."

"What did she say?"

"She wants you to call her back. But before you do, I need to tell you something. Let's walk."

"Why?"

"I can't think when I'm standing still." As he moved along the paved path beside the lake, static energy fizzed around him. "We were right to be worried about the police lights at the museum."

She kept pace with his long-legged stride, fearing the worst. "Is this about Ty Rivera?"

"He's dead."

Shocked by the unexpected news, she sucked in a sharp breath. Though she'd never actually met Rivera, she'd spoken to him on the phone and had an appointment this very afternoon. "An accident?"

"His throat was cut."

"How did—"

"You don't want to know," he said. "I don't mean to be blunt, but there's no time for a sensitive explanation. And you might want to brace yourself. From here on, the story gets worse."

When he unintentionally started walking faster, she nearly had to jog to keep up with him. "I'm ready."

"According to Logan, your mom met Ty Rivera for lunch. It's likely Gloria was one of the last people to see him alive." He shook his head. "Logan recognized her name from when I asked him to trace her credit cards. And he knows you have an appointment with Rivera."

She digested the information and immediately recognized the possible consequences. Gloria could be a murder suspect. "Is your brother going to arrest her?"

"He wants me to put him in touch with you and with Gloria."

She came to a halt, gazed across the lake where geese and ducks swooped and chased along the calm water. At the eastern end was the Band Shell and Pavilion, sunlit and glowing amidst a canopy of trees and lawns, which were still green in October. The scene was idyllic, but she was gripped by dread. This was the moment she'd feared, the moment when Shane had to choose between his law-abiding upbringing and her edgy family. "What are you going to do?"

"He's my brother, Mallory. I can't lie to him."

"What did you tell him?" She shot a nervous glance over her shoulder at the museum where police lights continued to flash. Shane had been guiding her in that direction. Did he intend to leave her in his brother's custody? Had he already decided to abandon her?

"I didn't lie," he said.

When he clasped her hand, she jerked away from him. Last night, she thought she'd finally found a man she could trust, but she was wrong. He'd betrayed her. "Let me go."

"I'll never hurt you, Mallory. Sure, I'd feel better if I could tell my brother the whole truth. And I'd welcome the police for backup. We're talking about murder here and need all the help we can get. You and I are running around with nothing but my Glock for protection, and I'm not a great marksman."

"But we have Elvis."

In spite of his tension, he laughed. "The dog is fierce."

She met his gaze. "What exactly did you say to Logan?"

"I sidestepped. When we were kids, I got out of fights by telling nothing while using a barrage of words. Here's how it works. One time I borrowed his favorite baseball glove without asking and left it at the park. I never actually lied to him but never admitted that I lost his dumb glove. After dinner, I crept out of the house and found it. All was cool."

The current situation was far more complicated than a piece of missing sports equipment. "How much did you say about Mom?"

"I could honestly say that I've never met the woman. Then I tap danced around the topic, avoided telling him about the Teardrop and our investigation. I didn't even mention that I was in Denver, probably standing a couple of hundred yards away from where the murder took place."

A gust of relief whooshed through her. She stepped toward him and collapsed against his chest, welcoming the shelter of his arms. "What did you tell him about me?"

"He already knows about your search for Gloria and has spoken to the Aspen sheriff and the Pitkin County sheriff. Until this is over, we've got to avoid all the local cops."

"I wish it didn't have to be like this. I had hoped that the first time I met your family, we'd be sharing a dinner, reminiscing over pot roast and mashed potatoes."

"Wrong picture. My family are decent people, but we're not a wholesome Norman Rockwell painting."

"Who?"

"As part owner of an art gallery, you ought to know." He tightened his embrace. "We'll head back to Aspen. Gloria mentioned to Walter that she was returning home."

"Should we drive?"

"Yeah." He kissed her forehead. "I want to keep my

Glock with me, so we can't fly commercial. And I can't count on my buddy with the helo."

She glanced back at the museum. "It's probably for the best that I can't talk to your brother. I mean, there isn't really anything I can tell him about the murder."

"Begging to differ." Using his thumb and forefinger, he lifted her chin so she was looking up at him. "Tell me, Mallory. Who do you think killed Ty Rivera?"

"Conrad Burdock is a shady character. And Felix told us that Mom suspected my father was following her. He could be a murderer."

"Those are two suspects my brother doesn't have. You know a hell of a lot more than my brother."

But she didn't want to know. She wished her mind could be blissfully empty of all these terrible details of what had happened long ago before she was born. Her lighthearted mother had been an abused wife. She'd stolen a fortune in precious gems and changed her identity. Mallory had to wonder if she'd ever contacted her birth parents. Did Gloria have brothers and sisters? Someday, Mallory might wake up to find she had a dozen cousins. *But I can't complain*. Throughout her life, Mallory had enjoyed being with Mom, who was fun and funny, always attentive and encouraging. She'd made a great single mother. The best. And she wanted to stay in that world where they were happy and…innocent.

She wanted to build her future with sweet, sensual fantasies about her and Shane, joined together in the shower, talking and laughing. She longed for a real relationship, maybe more, maybe children. Ironically, she knew that Gloria would adore him—the man who claimed that he'd never hurt her. Deeply, deeply, deeply, Mallory wished she could follow this beautiful new path.

THE RENTAL CAR wasn't nearly as comfortable as Shane's Navigator, but Mallory was glad to be leaving the city and zipping along I-70 into the foothills, leaving rush hour behind. Denver was great, but Aspen was home. Before she made her phone call to Gloria, she needed to organize her thoughts. First, she needed to know what kind of arrangements Mom had made with Ty Rivera. Second, Gloria was undoubtedly returning to Aspen to pick up the Teardrop, and Mallory needed to know where she'd hidden it.

She glanced over at Shane. "You're sure Fordham recognized Mr. Sherman."

"Absolutely. Fordham even did his own parody of the way Drew Sherman talks. Phony-baloney, if you know what I mean."

"Are we thinking that she left the Teardrop with him for safekeeping?"

"It's a place to start looking, assuming she won't tell you."

The third thing she ought to bring up with Mom was Hannah Wye, the attorney. Mallory didn't know if Hannah was a legit lawyer or a flaky artist who dabbled in lawsuits. Gloria was going to need a criminal attorney to defend her against possible murder charges as well as the whole faking-her-death thing.

Last but not least, Mallory had to convince Mom to tell her where she was. She and Shane could pick her up and eventually turn herself over to law enforcement. Though Gloria had spent the past twenty-six years hiding from the authorities, that had to change. The murder of Ty Rivera sounded an alarm that couldn't be ignored. *Danger, danger, danger*. Someone—possibly Burdock, possibly her father or maybe even Amber—was willing to slash a man's throat to get what they wanted. If they got ahold of Gloria, it would be light's out.

In the meantime, she and Shane would keep Mom safe. Again, she looked toward him. Though she didn't trust him one hundred percent, she was beginning to depend on him. "Somehow, we've got to make her come with us so we can protect her."

"I have an idea."

"Shoot."

"Back in the old days when I had fans and groupies, especially in Aspen, I sometimes needed a place to go where I could be totally alone. I bought a tiny cabin in the middle of nowhere. It came in handy when I was in recovery and didn't want anybody to see me limping around."

"You have a secret hideout?"

He shrugged. "Call it a safe house. We can take Gloria there and barricade the doors."

With her seat belt fastened, she couldn't lean close enough for a real kiss. So she settled for stroking his cheek. "You're a genius."

"I know." Shane handed her a phone. "Call your mom. I already plugged in the number that Walter gave me. You can talk as long as you want on this. It's a prepaid mobile phone."

"A burner. Why do you have one?"

"I have several. They came with my how-to-be-a-great-private-eye kit," he said. "Burners are handy for all sorts of things. Use it. Then pitch it. Untraceable."

She dialed the number and listened to six rings before

Gloria answered with a squeaky, nasal voice that wouldn't fool anybody. *"Bonjour,"* she said, "this is zee wrong number."

"Mom, it's Mallory. We need to talk."

"Me first," Gloria said without the phony voice. "I called to let you know that I finally have everything worked out. By this time tomorrow, I'll be able to explain everything."

Tomorrow might be too late. Hoping to get Mom's attention, Mallory held her reaction and switched focus. "Does Mr. Sherman have the Teardrop?"

"How on earth did you figure that out? I'm impressed or, as Drew Sherman would say, I'm hob-nob-gobsmacked." She gave a raucous chuckle. Clearly, Gloria thought she'd solved all her problems and was sitting pretty. "Did his son tell you? I didn't know you and Josh were still friends."

"Are you going to pick up the diamond from him?"

"Well, I can't do that until tomorrow morning when the bank opens. He put it into his personal safe-deposit box, and it requires two keys to open the vault."

"And then what happens?"

"I made arrangements with a guy at the Museum of Nature and—"

"Ty Rivera," Mallory said. "He's a friend of Felix's."

"Well, you know everything, don't you? Anyway, Ty set me up for a meeting with an important person from Sierra Leone to hand over the Teardrop."

"I need details, Mom." Rivera hadn't been killed for a vague indication of a handoff. "What is this important person's name? Does Felix know him or her? Where will the meet take place? When?"

"None of those things are any of your concern."

As if she could keep from being concerned? Late afternoon was fading into twilight, a hazardous time to be on the road. "Are you driving, Mom? Maybe you should pull over while we talk. I have some bad news."

"Not about Amber, I hope. I've always felt terrible about leaving her behind. Do you think she can ever forgive me?"

Not unless you give her the diamond. "Just pull over."

"I could say the same to you, Mallory. Are you driving?"

"I'm not behind the wheel."

"Who is?"

Now wasn't the time to introduce her to Shane, though she'd technically already met him by phone the last time they talked. "Please, listen to me. I don't want you to drive while you're distracted."

"I'm hanging up now."

"Wait, wait, wait. Okay, we'll do this your way." *Was there ever any doubt that Gloria would wear me down?* "So, Mom, answer this for me. After all these years of hiding, why are you suddenly willing to trust the word of Rivera?"

"Recommendations from other gem dealers," Gloria said.

"Like who?" Despite an effort to stay cool, Mallory's temper was rising. "Fences? Thieves? Conflict diamond warlords? Criminals?"

"Don't be overdramatic, dear. Felix knows Rivera and can vouch for him."

Mallory didn't want to lapse into a futile argument but needed for Gloria to understand. "I want to help you. There's no need to do this by yourself."

"I have everything under control."

"Ty Rivera is dead. Murdered."

"No."

Gloria gasped. Mallory cringed. Maybe, just maybe, she finally realized what kind of risk she was taking. "Are you okay?"

"We had lunch together. I thought he might be flirting with me but more likely he was thinking about the Teardrop. Damn that stone. It brings nothing but pain and sorrow." She rambled, avoiding the difficult topic. "The food wasn't even that good. Some limp salad. Ty had the vegetarian chili."

"I get it. You ate at the T-Rex Café in the museum." Gently, Mallory reined her in. "There were witnesses. You were one of the last people to see Rivera alive."

"You make it sound like I'm a suspect."

"It might be smart to put a good attorney on retainer. Does Hannah Wye handle criminal cases?"

"Don't be ridiculous. I'm not a murderer."

"You can't pretend like this isn't happening." Desperation crept into her voice. "Mother, you're in danger."

"I can handle it."

"Let me help." She glanced over at Shane. "I know a safe house where you can hide out until this is settled. Where can we meet in Aspen?"

"That's not going to happen, especially not now. I'm not going to put you in danger."

Mallory flopped back against the seat. *Talk about a giant reversal.* All this time, she'd been protecting Gloria. Now the tables turned. "Trust me."

"You listen to me and pay attention. It's true that I messed up with Amber, but I did a good job raising you, and I'm not going to let a murderer attack you. Stay away from me. I forbid you to contact me again."

Taken aback, Mallory stared at the phone. Her mother wasn't the type of parent who forbade her from doing anything. When Mallory wanted to go on an overnight trip or skip school or try vodka, Mom had stepped aside and allowed her to make her own mistakes. Gloria was a cool mother, not the type to tell her she couldn't do something.

Gloria continued, "My way of parenting worked. You graduated at the top of your class with scholarship offers for college. You were popular, mostly drug-free and strong. Now, I'm giving you an order. Leave me alone."

"Don't you dare forbid me. I'm not going to stand around with my thumb up my nose while some diamond hunter attacks you."

"Goodbye, Mal. I love you."

The phone went dead.

"She hung up on me." Not a big surprise. Mom had decided not to cooperate and nothing would change her mind. Mallory looked to Shane. "Now what are we going to do?"

"Gotta find her," he said.

"In Aspen? Offhand, I can think of dozens of places she could hole up until tomorrow morning when the bank opens. Not to mention that there might be a killer tracking us down. As if that isn't enough, the police are going to be looking for us." One complication piled on top of another. "How are we going to search?"

"We have a secret weapon."

"What's that?"

"He ain't nothing but a hound dog." Shane tapped the side of his nose. "But Elvis can find anybody, anywhere."

Even when they don't want to be found.

Chapter Seventeen

By the time they drove the rental car into Walter Pulaski's gated community and parked in his triple driveway, twilight had merged into dark. The huge marble sculpture of a woman emerging from the snow in his front yard with her head tilted back and her arm extended was artistically lit. Revolving lights created the illusion that her long hair rippled in the breeze as her delicately sculpted hand reached for the stars. The effect mesmerized Shane. He thought the statue's impossible quest to grasp the heavens made her oblivious to the mundane concerns of everyday creatures. Much like Gloria, Pulaski's muse.

Starting twenty-six years ago, Mallory's mom had made a series of bad decisions. The latest—refusing their help—was risky for her and for them. Though he understood her pride and her unshakeable belief that she had life under control, her current decision impacted Mallory. He couldn't let things slide or pretend nothing was wrong, which seemed to be Gloria's default position. He needed to find her and the Teardrop.

Right now, things were about to get a whole lot better because Elvis would be rejoining the team. While in Denver, Shane had missed his canine partner. As he and Mallory walked up the shoveled sidewalk to the front door, he saw the black Lab bouncing up and down as if his feet were on springs. At the high point of each bounce, he peeked through the beveled glass window in the door.

As soon as Pulaski unlocked the door, Elvis leaped outside. Though the dog was trained not to jump on people, Shane had a signal to override that command. He went down on his good knee and held out his arms, which meant it was okay for Elvis to dive into his embrace, to lick his face and make all kinds of weird growls and joyful yips. His sleek furry body wriggled happily against Shane's chest. Was there anything better than the greeting from a loyal dog after being apart? Still excited, Elvis danced in a circle, shaking his shoulders and wagging his tail like a metronome gone wild.

Mallory copied Shane's pose, and Elvis pounced on her. Since she wasn't very large, the dog toppled her into the snow beside the shoveled walk. She let out a giggle and a shriek. Unapologetic, he stood over her, nudging her with his nose and licking while she laughed.

"I missed you," she said to the dog. "Our trip to Denver was terrible."

"Sorry to hear that," Pulaski said. "Come on in. I've got a pot of beef stew and homemade bread."

On the front stoop, Shane caught a whiff of the stew from the kitchen and realized that the sisterly fight had caused him and Mallory to skip lunch. "Great timing. I'm hungry."

She gave Pulaski a giant hug. "I'm so glad to see someone I can trust."

Could she? Shane had slotted Pulaski in the "good guy" column but intended to be careful in what he said and did.

The multi-million-dollar diamond made a powerful incentive for switching over to the dark side.

Before he entered the house, Shane glanced over his shoulder at the street and considered the imminent threat. Though Pulaski's house featured top-notch security and he employed two husky assistants who could also act as bodyguards, danger still existed. Pulaski's friendship with Mallory's mom was well-known. He'd been pulling that lady out of trouble ever since she moved to Aspen.

Following him inside, Shane asked quietly, "Any other contact from Gloria?"

"Only the one phone call to Mallory's number. You?"

While Mallory and Elvis went to the kitchen to dish up bowls of stew, Shane confided, "I suppose it won't come as a shock to you that she's being unreasonable."

"I'd expect no less." In a thoughtful gesture, he stroked his white beard. "Can you give me a recap?"

"She made an arrangement with Ty Rivera at the Museum of Nature and Science. Gloria was the last person to see him before he was killed—his throat slashed by an ancient Mesoamerican obsidian blade from one of the exhibits."

Pulaski exhaled a sigh. His eyes were weary and worried. "Are the police looking for her?"

"My brother's a cop. The Denver PD views her—and Mallory—as persons of interest in the murder. The Aspen police and Pitkin county sheriff have also been informed."

"Sounds to me like you and Mallory have nowhere to turn." He took his usual seat at the head of the table where a half-full snifter of brandy awaited his return. "What's next?"

"First, we eat. And then we locate Gloria and try to talk sense into her."

"Good luck with that."

When Mallory returned to the dining room with a bowl-ful of stew and a chunk of fresh bread, Elvis made his presence known. He rubbed against Shane's leg and looked up at him with a happy smirk as if to say, "Glad you're back. Don't ever leave me again." Then he went to Pulaski and rested his chin on the old man's knee.

As soon as she was seated, she asked, "Uncle Walter, how well do you know Felix Komenda?"

"The guy who sent those letters to Gloria? We've met. On one of his visits to Aspen, I spent some time with him. A lean handsome man," he said with a sigh. "And a so-phisticated artist who modernizes themes and colors from folk art. On his chest, he has a tattoo of a kapok tree that stands in the middle of Freetown. When I asked about it, he told me the Cotton Tree is over two hundred years old and symbolizes freedom for the Black settlers of Sierra Leone."

Shane didn't ask how Pulaski knew what tattoo im-printed Felix's bare chest. These guys were entitled to their privacy, and Shane liked both of them. But he couldn't ig-nore the many connections Felix had with the Teardrop. He raised Amber, worked for her father and corresponded with Gloria. With roots in Sierra Leone, he might know Burdock, Ty Rivera and the mysterious person who would help Gloria deliver the diamond to those who needed it.

Felix seemed like a "good guy," but Shane had to won-der. He looked toward Mallory. "Why are you asking about Felix?"

"Trying to get my bearings and figure out what we do next. I'm thinking we should first visit Mr. Sherman."

Pulaski gave her a disbelieving look. "Drew Sherman the banker?"

In the kitchen, Shane filled a bowl with chunky beef stew containing potatoes, carrots, onions, parsnips and peas. He listened to Mallory explain how Fordham had seen Gloria with Sherman at the airfield. It seemed obvious that she'd given the Teardrop to the banker. But why hadn't he contacted the police when Gloria was reported missing? At least he should have told Mallory. Why was Sherman keeping that secret? Though it was hard to believe a man who claimed everything was hunky-dory could be part of a plot to steal the jewel, Shane needed to treat Sherman with the same level of suspicion as everyone else.

He took his place at the table opposite Mallory and dug into the hearty stew. He gave a long low moan that must have sounded like one he'd make while having sex because Mallory was staring at him with her eyebrows raised and a smart-aleck grin. He allowed pleasant memories to penetrate his mind and arouse his senses before speaking. "I don't think we should bother with Sherman tonight. Gloria said that he promised to keep the Teardrop in his personal safe-deposit box at the bank. Which means he can't access it until tomorrow."

"He might have lied to Gloria."

"Sure, but if he's being a loyal friend and hiding it for her, why lie? On the other hand, if he's aware of the danger associated with the gem, why keep it at his home?"

She dipped the heel of her bread into the last of her stew, soaking up the dark, rich mushroom gravy. "Where should we start searching?"

Though he wanted to drive out to the airfield and pick

up his Navigator, the anonymous rental vehicle offered more protection. "Your mother mentioned seeing Raymond DeSilva at the Hotel Jerome. Let's go there and show his photo around."

"Hold on." Pulaski waved his hands. "I thought DeSilva was dead."

"So did we," Mallory said. "Amber lied."

"A terrible deception. I'm so sorry, dear heart."

"It's just as well." She tossed her head and lifted her chin. "Amber and I want very different things. She's after the big payoff for selling the diamond, and I feel that it ought to be returned to Sierra Leone to benefit the people."

Elvis circled the table and sat by her, offering a sure signal of approval. Shane agreed. As far as he was concerned, the Teardrop was cursed until it was used for good.

THE MIDSIZE RENTAL sedan didn't meet with Elvis's approval. Shane had spoiled the diva dog by refurbishing the back of the Navigator into a cozy nest with an excellent view. Though he'd spread a couple of towels to protect the rear seat upholstery, Elvis couldn't get comfortable. Growling to himself, he paced from one side to the other and nudged the windows, an indication that the only way he'd like this mode of transportation was if he could hang his head out the window.

"Not gonna happen, buddy." Sitting behind the steering wheel, Shane craned his neck around to see into the back. "It's too cold to drive with the windows down, and we're supposed to be incognito. Everybody in town knows you."

Mallory reached between the seats to scratch the parallel worry lines between the Lab's eyebrows, if he'd had eyebrows. "You're too famous for your own good."

Elvis already wore his harness emblazoned with the words *service dog*, which ought to be enough to get him in the front door when they reached the downtown hotel. Shane had already called ahead to make sure his friend was working tonight and would be willing to talk about current guests. This interview couldn't be conducted over the phone since Shane had identification photos to show from his computer. The bad guys probably checked in using aliases.

He'd debated with himself about whether or not Mallory should be involved in this part of the investigation. His number one priority was to protect her from certain danger. If the police were involved, she'd be tucked away in a safe house with armed guards protecting her. Instead, they were on their own with little more than Shane's two Glocks to hold off the threat.

Leaving her with Pulaski hadn't been an option. Not only would she have refused to sit quietly on the sidelines, but Shane didn't feel right about putting her trusted old friend in peril. As he drove through the plowed but still snow-covered streets of Aspen toward Hotel Jerome, he considered asking her to stay in the car while he went inside. *Not a good solution.* If Mallory was alone, she made an easier target.

"I have a question," she said.

"Shoot."

"Well, I would. But I don't have a weapon." From the corner of his eye, he saw her smile before she said, "Har-de-har-har."

"Are you channeling Drew Sherman?"

"Making a point," she said. "You have two guns. One

in a shoulder holster and the other hooked to your belt. I should have one of those in my pocket."

Inwardly, he groaned. "You told me Gloria didn't approve of firearms. Have you ever even held a gun before?"

"I'm not a hunter, but I know the basics."

"I'll keep that in mind. For right now, I need you to concentrate on managing Elvis." Actually, the dog made a more intimidating weapon than a Glock. "His attack command is *g-e-t-e-m*. Drop his leash, point, give the command and watch this handsome rock star turn into Cujo."

At the hotel, he pulled up to the valet station, handed the guy a twenty and told him they'd be back in fifteen. Mallory held the leash as they entered the lobby. Hotel Jerome didn't have the high ceilings and ornate design of the Brown Palace, but the historic Aspen hotel had a uniquely Western charm with polished wainscoting, heavy furniture and mounted trophy heads of elk and deer on the walls. With Mallory and Elvis at his side, Shane approached the reception desk and nodded to his friend Kevin, who motioned for them to come around the desk into the office area. The front-desk clerk stood taller than Shane's six feet two and had an athletic build. Years ago, he'd come to the mountains as a ski bum. Now this was his home. He greeted Shane, gave Mallory a hug and hunkered down to shake paws with Elvis.

"We appreciate this," Shane said.

"Always happy to help my favorite private eye and his fur-ball sidekick." Kevin straightened his vest and stood. "What do you need?"

"These guys might be registered under fake names." He opened his tablet screen and showed the first photo.

"That's Felix Komenda. I don't remember seeing him

recently, but he stays here often. He's friends with Gloria. Good tipper." He gave Mallory a skeptical look. "I can't believe he did something bad."

"Neither can I," she said. "We're just covering all the bases."

Shane held up a photo of Raymond DeSilva, a handsome older gentleman with a groomed mustache and silver streaks at his temples. "How about this guy?"

Kevin nodded. "Yeah, he was here for a couple of days. Checked out this morning."

The timing struck Shane as being too coincidental. Amber and her father had arrived in Aspen at approximately the same time. "What name was he using?"

"I remember because it was an obvious alias. Raymond Chandler, like the guy who wrote the detective books. You know, Phillip Marlowe."

"I didn't know you were a reader."

"At night, it gets boring," Kevin said. "And I like a good *noir*."

Shane pulled up a snapshot he'd found of Conrad Burdock. Since Mallory actually saw Burdock, she had verified the identification. Hadn't been an easy search. Supervillains, like Burdock, didn't like to have their pictures taken. He showed the screen to Kevin.

"Whoa, you know him?" Kevin's surprise was genuine. "The ambassador?"

"Tell me more."

"He checked in five days ago with an entourage—all big guys who looked more like bodyguards than butlers. The ambassador is all class but friendly. Nice to the little people. He stopped at the desk himself to pick up a special delivery package and opened it right there. A bunch of muffin-type things from a bakery in Denver. The ambassador called them street cakes and offered me one."

"Nice," Shane said. Was Burdock a supervillain or a superhero?

"Totally delicious. And he's a handsome dude. In this job, I see a lot of beautiful people, but the ambassador was right up there at the top. His dark brown Versace jacket fit perfectly, and he had a humongous diamond pinkie ring."

"A diamond?"

"Huge diamond."

Shane exchanged a glance with Mallory before looking back at Kevin and asking, "Where is the ambassador from?"

"Someplace in Africa. He has a lapel pin with a blue, white and green flag. And a circle pin with a stylized picture of a tree."

"Freetown," Mallory said. "The Cotton Tree. And those are the colors of the Sierra Leone flag."

"Is he here?" Shane asked.

"Not on a Friday night. He and his entourage are out and about. The guy who pays all their bills asked where they could hear jazz and eat sushi. I made reservations. He tipped me a hundred bucks and passed on his thanks from the ambassador. Like I said, a class act."

And maybe a murderer.

Chapter Eighteen

Back in the rental car on their way to pick up the Navigator from the airfield where Shane had left it, Mallory hunched over the computer. In spite of occasional jostling in the passenger seat, her search of the internet quickly led to the ambassador to the United States from Sierra Leone. His multi-syllable British-sounding name wasn't Conrad Burdock, but his face belonged to the guy she'd met at the gallery.

"Everybody's got some kind of false identity." She leaned back in her seat and stared through the windshield at the cloudless night. "My father is pretending to be somebody else. My mother faked her death, and I can't begin to guess where she came up with the Gloria Greenfield name."

"Suits her," Shane said. "I've never met her, but the name makes me think of something bright and natural."

"That's her, all right." She continued her list of phony names. "The ambassador from Sierra Leone—with the last name of Lewiston-Blankenship—has his own alias."

"The first time we heard about Burdock was through Amber, right?"

"She claimed that he'd killed our father. Obviously, not

true. She also said the guys who chased us away from Reflections worked for him which he denied. Another lie?"

"Absolutely," Shane said. "Kevin's description of an entourage built like bodyguards fits the thugs in ski masks who came after us and made bullet holes in my car."

"An ambassador." She shook her head and sighed. Truly, there was no one or nothing she could trust.

"The fact that Burdock and your father were both staying at Hotel Jerome at the same time is suspicious. They might be working together."

"How does Amber fit into that picture?"

"She doesn't." He shrugged, but his tense grip on the steering wheel told her he was anything but nonchalant. "I think Amber is about to get the rug pulled from beneath her feet. One or both of those men are going to cut her out of the profits when they sell the Teardrop."

Mallory almost felt sorry for her sister. Amber dreamed of a vast fortune, enough wealth to live like a princess. Not much chance of that. By placing her trust in her slimeball father, she'd bet on the wrong horse.

Not that Mallory's loyalty to Gloria had paid off. "Do you think the ambassador is the person Ty Rivera arranged for Mom to meet?"

"I do."

She noticed how he kept checking the rearview mirrors, making sure they weren't being followed. Fortunately, there weren't many headlights on the road to the airfield. The major activity on a weekend would be in town with everybody yakking about the new snow and wondering when the slopes would open. The Hotel Jerome had just been starting to get busy when they left. "If Ty Rivera was working with the ambassador, why was he killed?"

"Loose ends," Shane said. "Rivera was a witness. Maybe he knew the ambassador was after the Teardrop and expected to receive a payoff. Or maybe Rivera honestly believed a high-ranking official from Sierra Leone would do the right thing. Either way, he'd be a liability…if and when these crimes come to light."

"What do you mean? What crimes?"

"Let's start with fraud. Who owns the diamond and how can they prove it? There's smuggling involved to get the jewel in and out of the country. Don't even get me started on political ramifications. In the worst-case scenario, violence erupts and somebody else gets killed. I don't need to remind you that the ambassador's thugs shot at us."

"Do you think they'd hurt Mom?"

A long moment of silence stretched between them. In a quiet voice, he said, "Yes."

Deep in her gut, she knew he was right. Her mother could be killed. Mallory's eyes squeezed shut. She turned off the computer and clenched her fingers into fists, holding onto fragile hope. Sensing her distress, Elvis poked his nose between the front seats and bumped her elbow, demanding a pet. She loosened her hand to stroke the soft fur on his head. The warm friendliness comforted her, though she was far from calm.

From the moment Gloria went missing, Mallory feared dire consequences, even before she knew the whole story. Mom shouldn't have gone off half-cocked, should have looked to Mallory for help, should have engaged a lawyer. Was it too late to make things right? "What can we do?"

A few more ticks of silence passed. "I know you don't want to hear this, but the murder of Ty Rivera makes the threat to your mom even greater. We should call the police. I can coordinate their actions through my brother."

"Sensible."

"Safe."

But she couldn't betray Mom's confidence, couldn't be the person to send her to prison. "Before we call in the cops, we have to find her."

"The cops can make our search easier. When you first discovered she was missing, you activated the entire town of Aspen, from forest rangers to the Pitkin County sheriff."

"That effort didn't turn out well," she reminded him. "I know Mom better than anybody else. With a little help from Elvis, I can find her."

He turned left onto the road that led to the hangars at the airfield. "I'm worried about you, Mallory. You could be next on the list of people who need to be eliminated."

Once again, his reasoning made sense. Another complication she didn't want to face. "I hadn't considered the threat to myself."

"I have." He parked beside his Navigator and killed the engine on the rental sedan. "You're the main thing I think about."

She unfastened her seat belt and twisted in her seat to embrace him. The midsize sedan had insufficient room for maneuvering, and Elvis got between them. But she managed to join her lips with his. His mouth tasted warm and familiar but exciting at the same time. Fighting the dog for Shane's attention, she pressed her upper body against his.

Though she didn't agree with everything he'd said, she understood his logic. And she actually appreciated his law-abiding attitude. Gloria had taught her the difference between right and wrong. "She's not really a criminal."

"A lot of decent people step outside the rules from time to time." He kissed her again. "Most of them don't get involved in international intrigues with twenty-million-dollar gems."

"Go big or go home." That was what Mom always said.

Elvis disentangled himself from their threesome, bounded into the back seat and ran to the window. Peering through the glass at the Navigator, he raised his chin and howled like a coyote seeing the moon.

"I think he wants to go back to your car," she said.

"You bet he does. It's cozy, and he's got a great view. The Navigator is like home on wheels." He unfastened his seat belt and opened the car door. "Let's go find Gloria."

SHANE POINTED THE 4WD Navigator—a vehicle both he and Elvis loved—back toward town. Their starting place had to be Gloria's house. Neither he nor Mallory thought her mom would be dumb enough to make that her hideout, but they needed to pick up an article of her clothing for Elvis to sniff before he got into serious tracking.

In the passenger seat beside him, Mallory was making plans, listing places her mom liked to hang out, including the back room of her favorite restaurant, an ex-lover's house and a mountain cave at the bottom of the towering cliff beside Reflections. She mumbled, "I doubt she'll go there in this weather."

"Probably not, but don't scratch anything off the list." If they found Gloria, he could convince mom and daughter to abandon the lone-ranger act and go to the police. His brother would be hacked off at him for not leveling with him, but Shane's loyalty rested with his client. Even if he wasn't falling for Mallory, he'd follow her wishes, which seemed to be coming into sync with his. Finally, he'd almost convinced her to seek help from the police. With full-on protection from law enforcement, they might all survive.

As he drove into the hills outside Aspen, he watched Mallory in a series of quick glances as she combed her fingers through her hair, pulled it together in a long tail and twisted it into a knot on top of her head. He looked forward to the moment when he would unfasten her barrette and allow her blond hair to tumble over her creamy white shoulders.

"Almost there," she said. "You remember the house, right?"

"Hard to forget."

"Mom has wild taste, and that's an understatement. She claims to be utterly nonjudgmental with a unique ability to recognize when an art object or a painting is inspired or skillfully done."

Gloria's logic was shaky, but she must be doing something right. Reflections had been successful in a competitive market. "Tell me more about the house."

"When she bought the half-acre property twenty-six years ago, she got a great deal. It was just a small A-frame in a clearing surrounded by pines."

"You were a newborn."

"And she was raising me by herself. A single mother starting life over with a new identity. You'd think that would be enough for her to handle, but noooo. Gloria never could sit still. Almost immediately, she started adding rooms to the house. A totally new kitchen. A playroom for me. A giant bedroom with a walk-in closet for her. The A-frame was always under construction."

He remembered his first impression of Gloria's house. Chaotic but warm. "How did you feel about the constant renovation?"

"Why are you asking? Are you my psychotherapist?" She shrugged. "I don't mean to sound defensive, but it seems like I've spent most of my life explaining Mom to people."

Taking care of Gloria. He didn't say those words out loud because he wasn't a shrink and didn't want to criticize or analyze Mallory. If she was okay with her Mom revamping the house, so was he. "Home improvement and DIY is a way of life for a lot of people."

"Nothing wrong with that."

After he drove the scary stretch of road at the edge of a cliff and rounded a few more curves, they arrived. The porch light was on as well as other strategically placed lights to emphasize the multilevel architecture that sprouted with inconsistent styles, materials and colors. A deep purple wall melted into a rock silo bordered by a modernistic cedar cube. A barn-sized structure with a southwest wall of glass looked like an artist studio. The overall effect, even at night, was kind of breathtaking.

More than the wild design, he noticed light shining from one of the lower windows and most of the second floor. "Somebody's here."

She pointed to a rental car. A black SUV. "The ambassador?"

The other car had parked in the driveway, which had been shoveled earlier in the day. Shane pulled in behind the other vehicle. Moving cautiously in case anybody inside was watching, he approached the SUV and slashed the rear right tire with a four-inch blade he kept in his glove compartment. This time, nobody would be able to chase them. Then, he went to the back of the Navigator, opened the door for Elvis and gave a single command. "Quiet."

The Lab hopped out and stood beside him in a silent alert stance. In the brief time he'd been separated from Elvis, Shane had missed this level of unflagging obedience. "Good dog."

When Mallory stepped out of the door, he warned, "Don't slam it."

She carefully closed the door and tiptoed through the snow toward him. "Now might be a good time to give me a weapon."

"Not yet. You're in charge of Elvis. Do you remember the command for attack?"

"It's *g-e-t-e-m*."

"Follow me."

Reaching inside his parka, he drew the Glock from his shoulder holster and held it at his side as he followed a shoveled sidewalk to the front porch of what was probably the original A-frame. The front door showed no signs of being broken into, and the handle twisted easily. Unlocked.

Mallory stayed behind him with Elvis at her side. For her, this had to be a weird way to enter the house where she'd spent much of her life. The black-and-white-tiled foyer reflected another era—maybe the roaring '20s— with deco statues, ornate framed paintings and two small antique oak tables. Shuffling noises could be heard and seemed to be coming from the second floor. The intruder or intruders made a lot of noise, opening and closing doors and drawers. They didn't seem to care about being over-heard.

Exchanging a look with Mallory and with Elvis, Shane

raised his weapon and ascended the carved oak staircase to the peaked second floor of the A-frame where lavish Persian rugs covered the floors. A dusky rose paint covered the upper walls in a sitting room with a peaked ceiling at the top of the "A" and dark oak trim.

He followed the noises to a door beyond the original A-frame. If he had to guess, he'd say this was Gloria's bedroom with the walk-in closet. Before entering, he assessed the possibilities. With no idea how many people he might be facing or whether they had guns, he wanted to protect Mallory and Elvis. First disarm the enemy.

With a hard shove, he pushed the door. It swung wide and crashed against the wall. In a two-handed stance, Shane took aim. "Show me your hands."

The man stood beside a long dresser with the top drawer open. He wore a gray parka and a black knit cap. He whirled, dropped to one knee and raised his handgun. Felix!

Before Shane could react, Mallory shouted the command. "Get 'em, Elvis."

The dog flew past him. Though Felix lifted his hands in immediate surrender when he recognized Shane, Elvis had been given his order. He bashed into Felix, knocking him flat on his back. His jaws closed around the wrist that had been holding the gun.

"Down." Shane stalked across the room. "Down, Elvis. It's okay. You're a good boy."

The black Lab released his grip and lowered himself onto the floor with his chin on his front paws. A low growl rumbled in his throat.

Mallory rushed to Elvis and knelt beside him. She cooed and kissed the dog's smooth furry head, lightening his mood and causing his tail to thump. "Such a good boy. You're a star."

Straightening her spine, she glared at Felix. "And you're an ass. Did you break in? You could have been shot and killed."

"The dog is fierce," Felix said.

"Only when he needs to be." Shane studied the sleeve of Felix's parka where Elvis had chomped down just hard enough to tear the fabric. He'd been trained to take down the enemy and neutralize them, not to harm them unless commanded to do so. Shane had never needed to test his dog's lethal instincts.

"I did not break in. Gloria gave me a key a long time ago."

"Which still doesn't give you the right to come and go without permission." Mallory jabbed an index finger at his chest. "Have you spoken to her?"

"I have not. Many times, I tried to reach her by phone. She will not answer." His gaze darted around the room. "I must warn you. I did not come to this house alone."

Bad news. Shane looked over his shoulder toward the door. Of all the villains who could have accompanied Felix, the most toxic was the woman who strode through the door with her Beretta clutched in her manicured hand but not aimed at him. Her turquoise eyes—so like Mallory's—narrowed in a hostile glare.

"I'm not here to hurt anybody," she said, "especially not your stupid dog, but Ty Rivera's murder freaked me out."

Shane figured he might as well try to get some useful info from Mallory's sister. "Who do you think killed him?"

"That's obvious." She waved her gun impatiently. A

gesture that made him nervous. "The killer had to be Conrad Burdock. Or one of his hired thugs."

"You're referring to a man who was staying at Hotel Jerome with his entourage. The ambassador from Sierra Leone."

Felix's expression showed confusion and concern. Amber—who was a much better actress—protested loudly that she didn't know what he was talking about. "Burdock is a thief, a criminal. He followed me here and has been trying to—"

"No more lies." Shane had just about had it with Amber. "The ambassador checked into the hotel five days ago. I'm guessing it was shortly after Gloria visited the pawnbroker in Brooklyn. That's what inspired you to take up the chase for the Teardrop, and it must have done the same for Ambassador Lewiston-Blankenship."

"You're the liar," Amber said.

She pointed her gun at his chest, and Shane had to wonder if prodding Amber was the best strategy. "The man you call Burdock was in Aspen before you."

"Put down your gun and stop threatening us." Mallory stepped into the argument. "We know you arrived in town at almost the same time as your father, Raymond DeSilva."

"He's here?" Amber's fuss and bluster turned into tears. She lowered the gun. "He didn't tell me."

"Maybe you aren't his favorite person, after all."

"I don't have to listen to this." She swabbed moisture from her cheeks. "The Teardrop belongs to me."

"Is that why you're here? To search?"

"Duh! Isn't that why you're here?"

"We came to find something with Mom's scent. For Elvis to use in tracking."

"Cute." Amber pivoted and stalked away.

"She'll be back," Shane said to Felix. "I slashed one of your tires."

He exhaled a weary sigh. "Is it true? Burdock and the ambassador are one and the same."

"You knew Rivera, right?"

"Yes."

"Do you think he intended to refer Gloria to the ambassador?"

"I believe so," Felix said. "But Rivera is a respected gemologist. I find it unlikely that he would associate with Burdock. I fear this mistaken identity was engineered by someone very clever, namely Raymond DeSilva."

Shane had come to a similar conclusion.

Chapter Nineteen

Leaving Amber and Felix to deal with the flat tire at Mom's house, Mallory and Shane set out to track Gloria using a couple of T-shirts from the dirty clothes hamper. One featured a logo for Save the Whales. The other advertised the Jimi Hendrix Experience. Sitting in the passenger seat of the Navigator, she sniffed the unique scent of Gloria Greenfield, a mixture of oil paint, turpentine, the balsamic vinegar she often used on salads, lavender and a hint of patchouli. She hoped these faint fragrances would be enough to do the job. "Do you really think Elvis can find her?"

"Like I told you before, his sense of smell is ten thousand times more sensitive than ours." Shane drove toward a more populated area of Aspen. "I think we should start at your house. Gloria might seek places that are more familiar."

"Agreed. All she needs is a hideout until tomorrow morning when she can pick up the Teardrop from the bank."

"Is the bank open on Saturday?"

"Until noon," she said.

"What's going to happen after she has it?"

She'd been considering possibilities. Mom had held the Teardrop in her possession for twenty-six years and kept it, fearing the valuable gem would fall into the wrong hands.

Also, she realized that as soon as her story was known, she had to face the consequences. Mallory didn't like her answer but realized it had to be. "We go to the police."

"My brother can help."

"Maybe."

She appreciated that Shane didn't gloat. Instead, he seemed genuinely concerned about what would happen to Mom, a woman he'd never met. Mallory sighed. "I'll stand by her, no matter what. And I'll make sure she has a terrific attorney."

Though she hoped and prayed that everything would turn out all right, she couldn't count on happily-ever-after. Mom's vanishing act had overturned her life. She didn't know what to believe or which way to go. Nothing made sense. Her carefree mom had been an abused wife who undertook desperate measures to save herself. Unbelievable! Her past held so much sorrow. It seemed impossible for a loving person like Gloria to abandon her child. Which pointed out another big change in Mallory's life. She had a sister! And a father who was still alive and, by all accounts, an evil, vicious, malevolent human being.

She gazed through the darkness at Shane and allowed herself to smile. Meeting him signaled a change in the right direction. For a long time, the idea of a significant relationship didn't fit into her future. She'd put romance on the back burner, allowing it to simmer like an ex-boyfriend stew and never really expecting to find a mate. Then she'd tumbled into Shane's embrace, and she never wanted to leave. Happily-ever-after? Maybe so.

He parked the Navigator in front of her house. The porch lamp lit on a timer as it always did after sunset. Same for a lamp in the dining room. Her sidewalk hadn't been shoveled since this morning but was clear enough to walk on without slipping. There didn't appear to be any indication that Gloria had been here.

When Elvis climbed down from the back of the Navigator, he was all business. Shane poured water into a collapsible bowl for the dog and changed his harness to the search-and-rescue vest he'd been wearing the first time she saw him. He looked to Mallory as though awaiting some instruction.

"Okay, Elvis. Here's the deal," she said. "We're searching for Gloria. She's the person you were looking for at the base of the cliff near Reflections. I have a couple of her shirts. Hope that's enough to give you the scent."

Though she knew the Lab didn't understand most of the words she spoke, Elvis was a better listener than most people she knew. At least he paid attention.

While she unlocked the front door, Shane gave Elvis a chance to get familiar with Gloria's scent before entering the house. He also talked to the dog, much the same way she had. Elvis was the third partner in their little team, their family.

Shane gave the command. "Elvis, search."

Inside her house, she noticed that Shane held the Glock he'd taken from his shoulder holster, ready for return fire if they were attacked. She followed Elvis into the kitchen. On the countertop, she saw a newly opened package of chocolate and macadamia cookies, Mom's favorite. "Good boy, Elvis. That's a clue."

"He's good at his job."

"So are you," she said.

"Glad to hear you say that." He caught hold of her hand

and pulled her toward him. "I might need for you to write me a recommendation."

She glided toward him and wrapped her arms around his middle. With her head tilted back, she gazed into his golden-brown eyes. "I'd definitely recommend you. You're so good at so many things. Maybe too good. Maybe I shouldn't tell anybody else about you and hire you for a permanent position."

He kissed her, starting with a gentle pressure and escalating. At the same time, he tightened their embrace, until she felt like they were joined together. A happy ending and a new beginning at the same time.

The kiss ended, and he loosened his hold on her. With a grin, he said, "I'll take the job."

In the upstairs bedroom, they spotted a note in the same place she'd left her original "I'll be back" message. Mallory picked it up and read, "I love you, Mallie Monster. Don't want you to be hurt. Please, please, please don't try to follow me."

Mallory talked at the sheet of paper torn from a spiral notebook. "Too late, Mom. We're already on the trail, and we're going to rescue you. Whether you like it or not."

Shane signaled to her. "Let's go, Elvis is on the move."

The dog had returned to the front door where he stood, apparently waiting for them to catch up. "What's going on?" she asked. "Does he want to go out?"

"We need to follow him." Shane gave Elvis another whiff of Mom's shirts and opened the door. "I'm guessing Gloria left the house."

"Sharp deduction, Sherlock."

"Just try to keep up."

She found it hard to believe that Elvis could track

Mom's scent through the snow, but the dog kept his nose down and his tail pointed straight up. He moved swiftly while she and Shane struggled to keep pace. A gust of chill wind slapped her cheeks. Her boots tread carefully on the cleared but icy sidewalk.

Elvis led them down the street to the corner and from there to nearby Reflections. The parking lot hadn't been shoveled. Tire tracks of various sizes crisscrossed the snow, but no vehicles were parked there. It made sense for Mom to come here. Reflections probably would have been next on their list of places to search.

Elvis stood at the back door, looking at them over his shoulder. He gave a woof, as if telling them to hurry up.

Stumbling across the ridges of ice and snowdrifts, a sense of anticipation ratcheted up inside her. They might come face-to-face with her mother. No matter the final outcome, the drama that had started twenty-six years ago might finally grind to a conclusion.

Shane reached the door first, twisted the handle and shoved. It opened with a squawk, and Elvis immediately poked his nose inside. Mallory was right behind him.

"Wait," Shane said softly. "We don't know who or what is inside. I should go first. Down, Elvis."

The dog obeyed.

Though her heart revved at high speed, she agreed. Shane had the weapon and could protect them. She took a step backward and watched as he entered the mudroom where she'd changed from her boots to her green clogs almost every day. Using the Maglite from a shelf by the door, he checked out the room, then gestured for her and Elvis to follow him into the kitchen, where the overhead lights were already turned on.

Considering all the time she spent at Reflections, the place ought to be as familiar as her own home. But tonight, she saw the kitchen through different eyes, influenced by fear and apprehension. The pans hanging on a circular rack above the butcher-block table glinted brightly. An anxious, ceaseless hum from the refrigerator and meat locker stirred the air. The cutlery betrayed sharp edges. So many things could go wrong.

Elvis circled the prep tables in the kitchen, still sniffing. After a brief pause at the industrial-size oven, he went to the swinging door that led into the gallery and coffee shop. Out there, the gallery display area was huge, filled with nooks and alcoves. Following Mom's path, Elvis had his work cut out for him.

Before going through the swinging door, Shane whispered to her, "Lights on or off?"

"I can find my way around in the dark," she said, "and there ought to be enough glow from moonlight through the windows in the coffee shop."

"Elvis can search without lights, but can you?"

Good point. If Mom was determined to hide, she could make herself invisible in a shadowy corner. And if the bad guys had already arrived, they could be anywhere. "Lights on."

Passing through the swinging door, she flicked the switch that illuminated the coffee shop and the front area. The aroma of fresh brew told her that Gloria had been here. Three used cups sat in the middle of a table by the window. *Three cups.* She'd had company.

Bracing for the worst, Mallory hit the light switches by the front door. At first glance, nothing seemed out of place. Gloria might have already come and gone. If bad guys were here, she'd probably already alerted them by turning on the lights.

"Mom, are you here?" Her voice stayed at a conversational level. She cleared her throat and called out more loudly, "Gloria? Where are you? Mom?"

"Let's keep moving." Shane gave her a hug. "We'll find her."

Following Elvis saved them a lot of time. The dog didn't bother with the basement area where Mallory taught classes and paintings were stored. Elvis skirted most of the displays and went directly to the staircase leading to the narrow upstairs gallery outside the offices. From that vantage point, they could look down on the entire gallery.

With her boots clanging on every step, she charged up the metal stairs with Shane following. He'd moved from the front of the pack to the rear, and she noticed that he held his Glock at the ready and was constantly scanning, looking for threats. On the balcony, she leaned against the iron railing and looked down on the displays of paintings, photographs and sketches. She saw the garish sky paintings by Fordham, the pilot, and dainty watercolors of hummingbirds by Hannah Wye, the lawyer.

Mom was nowhere in sight. Elvis went down the corridor leading to offices but didn't pause outside any of the closed doors. Instead, the dog returned to the staircase and descended. His toenails clicked against the metal. He loped around the edge of the displays and returned to the coffee shop.

"Where's he going?" she asked Shane as she chased after the dog.

"Not sure, but we better follow."

Elvis paced back and forth in front of the tall window

panels that looked out on the sculpture garden where several of Uncle Walter's pieces were on display, ranging from an abstract grizzly bear to his trademark goddesses to several baby bunnies. Not that they could see details. The bright light in the coffee shop obscured the darkness beyond the windows, and moonlight didn't provide enough illumination to see anything more than vague shapes of white marble.

Squinting hard, Mallory could make out the two-foot-tall stone retaining wall at the edge of the garden, meant to be a barrier to protect unwary hikers from the seven-hundred-foot drop. In years past, it hadn't proven effective. At least five climbers had fallen to their deaths.

"What is it, Elvis?" Shane hunkered down to talk face-to-face with his search dog. "What did you find?"

The dog stood up on his hind legs and pressed his nose against the window glass. Something must be out there. At the far end of the windows near the coffee maker, Mallory flipped several light switches to activate spotlights in the sculpture garden. Much of the snow had melted on this western-facing patch of land that spread to the edge of the cliff.

She saw Gloria, tied to a life-size sculpture of Artemis, goddess of the hunt. A heavy rope around Mom's waist bound her to the white marble statue, but one hand had broken free. Visibly trembling, she reached toward the window.

Mallory gasped. Paralyzed by shock, her feet rooted to the floor. Her hand thrust forward as if she could break through the glass and rescue Mom.

Gloria's hand fell limply to her side. Her head drooped forward.

Chapter Twenty

Shane squeezed Mallory's shoulders and whispered, "Stay here with Elvis. I'll bring her inside."

She ought to go with him. This was her fight, not his. But it took all her strength to remain standing and not collapse in a heap on the floor. Her fingertips touched the ice-cold glass. Her gaze riveted on Mom. She must be so terribly cold, wearing only a light windbreaker and no mittens. When she raised her hand, her fingers clenched into a grotesque claw.

Stumbling toward a table, Mallory sank into a chair beside the window. Beside her, Elvis paced back and forth, expelling nervous tension, and then the dog halted and stood at attention, staring through the glass. Shane had entered the sculpture garden. Gun in hand, he made his way through the snow toward Gloria. He reached her and enfolded her in a hug. Mallory leaped to her feet, knocking over the chair where she'd been sitting. She couldn't hear what he was saying but knew he was speaking to Mom, offering reassurances.

Gloria nodded. Her eyes opened to slits. Mallory could tell that she was in pain. But still alive, damn it, she was still alive.

Shane had to put down his weapon to untie the knots

on the rope that held Gloria against the sculptured huntress with her bow and arrow. Though his fingers worked quickly, the minutes felt as slow as hours.

Gloria pointed. Shane twisted to look over his shoulder. A shot rang out.

A man dressed in black and wearing a ski mask aimed his handgun at Shane and Gloria. He must have missed because neither appeared to be injured. Shane dove to the ground to pick up his Glock. He rose to one knee, aimed and fired.

The masked man let out a yelp, loud enough for Mallory to hear through the triple-paned glass. He ducked behind a sculpture of a buck with an intricate eight-point rack and fired again.

Shane was on the move, drawing fire away from Mom, who had loosened the ropes and fallen to the snow-covered earth. Shane was in greater danger. From the time they first met, he'd warned her that he wasn't a sharpshooter, but he'd hit the attacker on the first try and now he nicked the antlers on the marble deer.

At the retaining wall on the edge of the garden, Shane angled for a better shot.

The masked man fired three times in rapid succession. Shane flinched. He was hit.

Helpless, she watched as his legs gave out. His body twisted. He fell over the retaining wall and disappeared from sight.

A guttural scream tore from her throat. With both hands, she banged against the window. Shane was gone. *This can't be happening.* She couldn't believe the cliff had claimed another victim, but she'd seen him fall. The man who shot him went to the retaining wall, looked over and shrugged. Shane's death meant nothing to him.

Elvis took off running. She didn't know which way he'd gone, couldn't remember the command that would stop him. Her only thought was revenge. If she couldn't have Shane back, she wanted to destroy the men who'd killed him. Under her breath, she muttered, "Get 'em, Elvis. Get 'em."

Through the window, she watched as another masked man lifted her mother and threw her over his shoulder like a sack of potatoes. Did he mean to fling her over the cliff?

"No!" she yelled. "Don't hurt her."

"Calm down," said a smooth baritone voice behind her. "We're not going to kill Gloria. That would be foolish. We need her to collect the diamond."

She turned and faced the man she'd known as Conrad Burdock. "You must be the Ambassador."

"I suppose I am." He went to the coffeepot and poured himself a mug. "It's unfortunate you discovered that connection. I can't have you talking to the Sierra Leone Embassy, can I?"

"You're a monster." Rage overwhelmed her sorrow. She wanted this man dead. "Why would you force my mother to stay out in the snow?"

"As I mentioned before, I don't want to kill Gloria, but I need her to work with me. She was being uncooperative, and I thought the cold might change her mind." He sipped his coffee. "This is a very nice brew."

"Choke on it."

"I'm so glad you're here. Your mother couldn't be convinced to work with me in spite of pain and cold. But I think she'll feel differently about threats to you, her darling daughter."

"You don't scare me."

"Then, you are a fool."

Mallory returned to the window. Elvis had gotten outside and positioned himself at the edge of the retaining wall where Shane had fallen. When one of the men in black approached the dog, Elvis bared his teeth and growled. The masked man backed off.

Elvis sat beside the wall. He tilted back his head and howled, long and low, commencing a loyal dog's vigil for his fallen master.

CLINGING TO THE granite face with one hand, Shane tried to recall details from when he had been here before, standing at the base of the cliff, looking up and thinking about the good old days when he'd guided groups on extreme skiing adventures that sometimes required him to do rock climbing. He had a knack for discovering the best route across a supposedly impassible wall of stone. If he hadn't been shot in the left shoulder, making his arm useless, and had been wearing better shoes for climbing, he could have easily maneuvered his way to the top. The snow didn't bother him. He was a skier and had dressed for the cold.

When he fell over the retaining wall, survival had been topmost in his mind. He'd skidded down the rock face over an outcropping that hid him from view from above. And he slowed his fall by grabbing every rocky protrusion and dangling root until he found purchase on a ledge about twelve feet from the lip and wide enough for him to stand flat-footed. He caught his breath and took stock of his situation.

In the garden above him, he heard Elvis setting up a howl. If he continued, one of the thugs would undoubtedly shoot him. Shane whispered the command, "Down, boy. Get down."

The howl ended immediately. Shane imagined the dog with his belly on the ground and his head resting on his front paws. But when he looked up, he saw the face of the black Lab peering down at him. "You heard me, Elvis. Get down."

He figured Elvis would prevent any of the masked men from coming closer to look for him. If they did, he wasn't helpless. True, he'd lost one of his guns in the fall. But he had another in his belt holster. Not that he wanted to get into a shoot-out. Blood seeped from his wound, and his shoulder felt numb. Plus, he didn't know how many of the enemy he'd be facing. Earlier, they'd encountered four attackers who worked for the ambassador, who made five. And there was Raymond DeSilva to consider.

The best option for his survival and that of Mallory and her mom meant calling for backup. Balancing precariously, he dug into his pocket and pulled out his phone. Activating the screen took some tricky maneuvering, but he got it working only to discover that his phone was fully charged but there were no bars. Not a big surprise. Not many people tried to make calls while dangling off the edge of a seven-hundred-foot cliff in the high Rockies above Aspen.

The irony struck him. Finally, he had a legitimate reason to call in the police, but his phone didn't work. If he hadn't been losing blood and feeling dizzy, he would have laughed.

Only one thing to do. He had to climb up a vertical rock face, crash into Reflections and overwhelm an unknown

number of armed thugs. Not the first time in his life that
he'd faced an impossible challenge. He could do it. He had
great motivation, and her name was Mallory.

MALLORY HUGGED HER MOM, sharing bodily warmth. Cold
as ice, Gloria shivered in her arms. Mallory took off her
parka and wrapped it around her. Still not enough. Gloria's fingers showed signs of hypothermia.

Mallory snapped an order at one of the men who worked
for the ambassador. "Go to the mudroom behind the kitchen
and get me a couple of blankets. And take off that stupid
ski mask. You look like a joke."

The ambassador nodded to him. "Do it."

She glared at him. "Leave us alone."

He swept a bow to Gloria. "I apologize for the incon-
venience, but I must insist on your cooperation. Where is
the diamond?"

Obstinately, Gloria shook her head.

"You're stoic when it comes to your own safety. But
how do you feel about punishment inflicted on your
child?" He snatched Mallory's long hair and yanked her
toward him. His arm snaked around her middle, and he
squeezed her upper arm so tightly that she yelped.

"Stop it," she snapped. "I'll be happy to tell you where
the Teardrop is."

"No," her mom said.

"It doesn't matter. He can't get to it." She faced the am-
bassador. "In a safe-deposit bank at Fidelity Union Bank.
The box belongs to Drew Sherman, a bank vice president.
If you threaten him, the police will be involved."

"I don't believe you."

"Call Mr. Sherman. Before you start threatening him,

consider the potential charges for bank robbery." She took the blankets from the guy who'd gone to the mudroom and tucked them around Mom's legs and shoulders. "By the way, did you murder Ty Rivera?"

He cleared his throat. "Certainly not."

"I'll rephrase," Mallory said. "Did you or one of your hired goons take a blade from a museum exhibit and slash his throat?"

"Why would anyone do such a thing?"

She knew the answer. "Because he thought you were the ambassador. But Gloria could identify you as your alter ego, Conrad Burdock, a criminal. I'm guessing you've used your political status to stay out of trouble with the law. Rivera could have ended that deception."

"And now," he said coldly, "you and Gloria know my secret. I arranged for the death of Ty Rivera."

Their chances for survival looked slim. She had to think fast, to come up with something that would cause him to hesitate and allow them to escape. "Earlier, you called me and suggested that we work together against Amber. Do you remember?"

He refreshed his coffee without offering any to her or Mom. "You should have accepted. There was no need for us to be enemies."

"We can still be partners."

She went to the coffee machine. Standing this close to the ambassador, Mallory struggled to restrain herself. There were weapons at hand. Hot coffee. The glass carafe. She might even find a knife in one of the drawers. But that revenge would be a short-lived pleasure. She kept herself under control, dumping the used grounds and brewing a fresh pot of coffee. While learning how to make sales at

Reflections, Mom had taught her about bargaining. Wait for the other person to speak first.

"What do you propose?" the ambassador asked.

"In the morning, Mom and I will go to the bank. You'll have to trust us to fetch the Teardrop and bring it to you. After that, we'll trust you to grant us our freedom."

"Why wouldn't you turn me over to the police?"

"Because we'd also go to jail. Mom stole the Teardrop." He still looked dubious, so she added, "And you'll pay us $200,000, which is about one percent of the worth."

The criminal alter ego of the ambassador understood her plan. "You have a deal."

"Now I'd like to take Mom home so she can rest and recover."

Mallory exchanged a grin with Mom. Truly, the acorn didn't fall far from the tree. She had no problem lying and making a deal with a criminal. She'd been born to it.

WITH A FINAL burst of strength, Shane hauled himself over the edge of the retaining wall and lay flat against it, breathing heavily while Elvis licked his face. The spotlights in the garden had been turned off, and he doubted anyone could see them in the shadows. The frozen night surrounded him. Snow permeated his clothing, but his shoulder wound flamed with dark wet heat. He was still losing blood. Not much time left before he passed out.

With his back leaning against the wall, he pulled the Glock from his belt holster. Staggering to his feet, he peered through the windows at the interior of the coffee shop. Mallory served a mug of coffee to her mom, who was swaddled in mismatched blankets. The ambassador, alias Burdock, strutted through the tables and chairs.

Shane saw two armed men who no longer wore masks. One of them must have been the guy he shot in the garden. Both his right leg and right wrist were bandaged. Shane figured the other two had been assigned to protect the front and back doors of Reflections, which meant he only had to get past one guard. And then what?

He took out his phone, glad to see the screen light up and he had bars indicating he could make a call. He tapped speed dial for his brother. The call went through.

Shane's strength was fading. He had to talk fast while his brain was still working and he made sense. "Logan, I'm at Reflections in Aspen. There are at least five men holding Mallory and her mom hostage. One of them probably killed Ty Rivera. I need backup."

"I'm on it, bro. I know the chief of police in Aspen. They'll be there pronto."

"Hostage situation," he repeated. "They can't go in with guns blazing."

"Got it," Logan said. "Mallory Greenfield is the woman you're working for, right? You care about her. I get it. Just don't do anything stupid."

"Count on it."

Shane ended the call and headed toward the rear door with Elvis following close behind. He didn't intend to do anything dumb but hoped to disarm the situation before the police arrived and everything got crazy. Mallory needed him. Now.

At the rear entrance, he saw a guy in a ski mask standing under the porch light, almost as though waiting for Shane to sneak up to him and knock him unconscious with the butt of his Glock, which was exactly what he did. Shane dragged the guy into the mudroom. In the masked man's pocket, Shane found a zip tie and used it to fasten his wrists behind his back. He turned the ski mask into a gag.

He crept through the kitchen and stopped at the swinging door. His shoulder wound began to throb. Still bleeding, he needed for this to be over. But he couldn't charge into the coffee shop while outnumbered and outgunned. He needed a distraction.

As if on cue, Amber slammed the front door and entered Reflections. In a loud near-hysterical voice, she demanded to know where the diamond was. "When will I get my share?"

He heard Gloria's faint voice. "My beautiful daughter, can you ever forgive me?"

"No. Never."

"I tried to do what was best."

"Best for you," Amber said. "Not for me."

He wondered where Felix was. He must have changed the tire and given Amber a ride here. Felix would be on Shane's side. He might even the odds.

Shane opened the swinging door enough that he could see when another person entered from the front. An older man, tall and handsome with silver streaks at his temples. Raymond DeSilva.

He swaggered toward the coffee shop and held his arms wide open. "Daddy's home."

Shane needed to take advantage of the chaos, but he didn't want Elvis involved. Even though the dog was trained to attack, he couldn't stop a bullet. "Stay," Shane ordered. "Elvis, you need to stay here."

The dog looked up at him with a wise, patient gaze that told Shane he understood. At the same time, Elvis gave a low dangerous growl. He was ready for a fight.

Shane crept toward the coffee shop where Amber argued with her father about how they should handle the situation. She seemed to think the plan hatched by Mallory and the ambassador would cut them out of the money. He was more inclined to take absolute control. When Gloria piped up, DeSilva whirled and slapped her hard, knocking her from the chair where she'd been huddled in blankets.

To his surprise, Amber responded, "It's true what Felix said about you. You're abusive, a predator."

"I'm the guy who paid your bills, little girl. You'll give me the respect I deserve."

"What happens if I don't? Are you going to hit me, too?" Amber whipped out her handgun. "Don't even think about it."

Mallory helped her mom back into the chair and placed herself in the middle of the argument. "Everybody settle down."

"Don't push me," DeSilva said with a sneer as he drew his gun.

"Go ahead and shoot," she confronted him. "You think you have a lot to lose, but it's only money. Tonight, I had everything taken away. My heart is broken. The man I love is dead."

Shane entered the coffee shop. His Glock aimed at DeSilva. "Drop it."

Before he could react, Amber fired her weapon. The bullet hit her father's gun, causing him to drop it. Amber laughed. "Daddy did an excellent job of teaching me how to handle firearms."

Shane turned his weapon on the ambassador and his men. "I've got you covered. No false moves."

From outside, he heard police sirens wailing. So much

for the subtle approach from the Aspen cops. The threat was enough to disarm the ambassador's men, who would all be arrested.

Mallory found her place beside him with his one good arm wrapped around her. Her incredible turquoise eyes filled with tears as she looked up at him. She whispered, "When I thought you were dead, I knew. You're the love of my life. I want to be with you forever."

"Yes," he said.

Forever and ever.

TEN MONTHS LATER in late summer, Mallory made good on her proposal. The wedding would be held in the sculpture garden at Reflections, where she thought she'd lost Shane forever. Mom had served a six-month sentence in a low-security prison in Englewood and would be on probation for five years. The light sentence came as a result of intervention from the Sierra Leone government, which was thrilled to once again have possession of the African Teardrop. The plans were to sell it and use the proceeds for schools. The new ambassador from Sierra Leone planned to attend the wedding.

Amber would serve as maid of honor. She still wasn't happy about losing out on the millions from the sale of the Teardrop but received a regular paycheck for opening a Reflections gallery in Brooklyn and handling uncle Walter's sculptures.

Logan Reilly would act as Shane's best man.

Standing at the edge of the garden, Mallory held Drew Sherman's elbow. He would escort her to the minister who stood before a bower of flowers. He leaned down to kiss her cheek. "You look real fancy-schmancy in that lacy white dress."

"Okey dokey."

Elvis in his red leather harness with the silver studs pranced down the aisle ahead of her, carrying their rings in a pouch. She had to admit that the dog was pretty cute, but her entire field of vision was filled by Shane, who looked amazing in his tuxedo. Shane Reilly was the best thing that had ever happened to her, and it was almost worth going through the tribulation of nearly losing her mother to find him. *Almost worth it.*

* * * * *